"Are you gonna see him tomorrow?" Christopher demanded, taking a sip of his Sprite and replacing the glass carefully on the table in front of him.

Aisha frantically searched through her mind for an excuse. There was always the truth, of course. That she intended to go to the prom with David and break up with him afterward. But obviously that would never go over. Why did Christopher have to put her through this? She'd already told him that she would break up with David. *When* she did it was inconsequential. As long as it was before the weekend anyway. "I don't know," she answered. "Maybe."

"Eesh," he said, gazing directly into her eyes. "When are you going to do it?"

She looked at him blankly. She didn't know exactly when.

Don't miss any of the books in
Making Out
by Katherine Applegate
from Avon Flare

#1 ZOEY FOOLS AROUND
#2 JAKE FINDS OUT
#3 NINA WON'T TELL
#4 BEN'S IN LOVE
#5 CLAIRE GETS CAUGHT
#6 WHAT ZOEY SAW
#7 LUCAS GETS HURT
#8 AISHA GOES WILD
#9 ZOEY PLAYS GAMES
#10 NINA SHAPES UP
#11 BEN TAKES A CHANCE
#12 CLAIRE CAN'T LOSE
#13 DON'T TELL ZOEY
#14 AARON LETS GO
#15 WHO LOVES KATE?
#16 LARA GETS EVEN
#17 TWO-TIMING AISHA

Coming Soon

#18 ZOEY SPEAKS OUT

MAKING OUT #17

Two-timing Aisha

KATHERINE APPLEGATE

AN AVON FLARE BOOK

This is a work of fiction. Names, characters, places, and incidents either are the product of the author's imagination or are used fictitiously. Any resemblance to actual events, locales, organizations, or persons, living or dead, is entirely coincidental and beyond the intent of either the author or the publisher.

AVON BOOKS, INC.
1350 Avenue of the Americas
New York, New York 10019

Copyright © 1996 by Daniel Weiss Associates, Inc.,
and Katherine Applegate
Published by arrangement with Daniel Weiss Associates, Inc.
Library of Congress Catalog Card Number: 99-94733
ISBN: 0-380-81119-7
www.avonbooks.com/chathamisland

First Avon Flare Printing: October 1999

AVON FLARE TRADEMARK REG. U.S. PAT. OFF. AND IN OTHER COUNTRIES, MARCA REGISTRADA, HECHO EN U.S.A.

Printed in the U.S.A.

WCD 10 9 8 7 6 5 4 3 2 1

For Michael

One

Aisha Gray heard footsteps approaching. She opened her eyes slowly, her lips moist and her body still tingling from David Barnes's kiss. *If that's my dad, I'm going to die of embarrassment,* she thought.

Peering into the black night, Aisha moved off the front porch and halfway down the small flight of steps leading up to the pedimented doorway of the Grays' bed-and-breakfast. She could see a shadow coming toward them, moving very quickly up the sloping road that led to Gray House.

Oh, my God! she realized in horror. *It's Christopher. What's he doing here?*

Then it dawned on her. That was what Christopher's postcard had meant.

You'll know soon enough what I mean when I say I've started to see everything in a new light, Christopher had written. He'd meant that he was coming home.

Aisha turned quickly to David. "I don't believe it," she whispered. "Did you hear that? My mom's calling me from inside." She took his arm and practically dragged him down the front steps of the porch, glancing nervously in Christopher's direction. He was just passing an arrow-shaped road sign that said Climbing

1

Way, which meant he was going to be knocking on her front door in eight seconds or less.

David stumbled on the bottom step. His brow was furrowed in confusion. "I didn't hear anything," he said.

"Well, uh . . . maybe you should get your ears checked." Aisha grimaced. *That didn't come out right.* "I mean, you'd better go *that* way to get to the road, because my mom might see you . . . and I'll get in big trouble." Aisha pointed to a dense clump of pine trees located several yards away, in the opposite direction from Christopher.

"But why—"

"Shhh! I'll talk to you tomorrow," Aisha said, giving him a push in the direction of the grove. "Bye." She ran up the steps as fast as she could. Her heart was pounding and her face felt hot and flushed.

Oh, God, I hope he didn't see us kissing, Aisha prayed, peeking out through the living room window. She was shaking all over, partly from David's kiss, partly from the close call, and partly from the anticipation of seeing Christopher again.

Christopher Shupe's heart slammed down to his feet. Under the porch light, just fifty yards away, Aisha was making out with some guy. Some *white* guy. She sure looked as if she was enjoying herself. For a moment Christopher stared at them, totally immobilized. Then he rushed forward. He would pound the jerk who was kissing his girlfriend.

Aisha was dragging the guy off her porch now, and Christopher stopped short. If he caught the guy, which it would be easy to do, what exactly would happen next? He tried to get a better look at him, but it was too dark to be able to make out his features. Suddenly the guy disappeared into the trees and Aisha ran into the house.

Christopher broke into a run. He stumbled over a rock in Aisha's driveway, but he quickly recovered and finally reached the front steps.

Breathing heavily and frantically turning in every direction, Christopher searched the front lawn for the creep who—just seconds before—had had his tongue in Aisha's mouth.

"Damn!" he said. He threw his fist into the side of a tree. "Bastard."

He took several deep breaths, trying to calm down, and paced back and forth in front of the inn. He could go around to the back and knock on Aisha's bedroom window, the way he used to do every morning. He could demand that she tell him what was going on.

Christopher sighed, remembering how he had stopped at Gray House every day at the end of his newspaper route and woken Aisha up for a good-morning kiss. Under the current circumstances, however, it was probably safer to ring the front doorbell. For all he knew, that creep had sneaked in through her bedroom window just now.

After a few minutes, when he felt a little less agitated, he stepped up to the front door. It swung open even before he had a chance to ring the doorbell, and Aisha's smiling face came into view.

"Christopher!" she said, giving him a warm hug. "What are you doing here?" She seemed genuinely happy to see him, and Christopher was confused. Was it possible that he had mistaken the situation? He frowned deeply. Absolutely not. There was no way anyone could explain away *that* lip lock.

Christopher pushed Aisha away roughly. "I saw the whole thing, Eesh," he said tightly. "Who *was* that guy?"

Her face fell. "I can explain," she said gravely. She opened the door a little wider and gestured for him to come inside. "Come in. Let's talk."

They sat awkwardly on opposite ends of an overstuffed sofa in the living room. Neither of them spoke for what seemed like an eternity. Christopher was still reeling from the shock of seeing Aisha, the love of his life, the woman he had proposed marriage to just five months earlier, playing tonsil hockey with someone else. It certainly hadn't taken long for her to get over him, he thought bitterly.

Finally Aisha cleared her throat. "It's not what you think," she began. "I mean, Da—that guy and I have been out a few times and all, but it's nothing like what you and I had."

Her eyes roamed the room as though she was trying to figure out what to say. Christopher remained grimly silent. His throat felt tight and dry as he waited for her to say something, *anything,* to excuse what he had just witnessed.

"I still love you, Christopher. And I never stopped loving you." Her lower lip began to tremble. "Please believe me."

Christopher felt his jaw relax a little. He moved closer to her and put a hand on her thigh.

"I've missed you so much," she said in a barely audible voice. "And I didn't know when—or if—I was going to see you again." Tears were streaming down her face.

The excitement he'd been feeling earlier in the evening as he hurried to tell Aisha his news suddenly returned to him. He had made so many plans, plans that involved Aisha, and he couldn't give up on that now. Christopher searched her familiar eyes for reassurance. "Eesh, I've made the decision to leave the army," he said. "I'm here for good."

Aisha's face brightened. "What?" she whispered.

"I quit."

"You mean you're AWOL?" she asked uncertainly.

Christopher laughed. "No. I got out on a medical excuse."

"But why?" she said, incredulous. "What about all your plans? What about college?"

He shrugged. "I'll go back to what I was doing before—working, saving up."

Aisha stared at him in disbelief.

"Eesh, I'm just not cut out for the army, and . . . and I've missed you, too," he said. "I want to be with you."

"Oh, Christopher," Aisha said, putting her arms around his neck and squeezing him. "This is so great—but, oh—"

"But what?"

"Christopher, I'm going to Princeton in the fall."

His heart sank. "Princeton," he repeated, making an effort to sound upbeat. "Wow. That's great, Eesh."

"But we can still stay together," she said reassuringly. "It's only eight hours away by car . . . we can visit each other."

Aisha's enthusiasm was contagious, and Christopher smiled in spite of his disappointment. They could work something out. Maybe he could even get a job down in New Jersey. "Yeah, it'll be okay," he said. "Anyway, for now I'm staying in a studio at the old apartment house on Leeward. You know, until I find a job and a better place to live."

"Wow . . . this really changes everything," Aisha said in a daze. "But you don't have anything to worry about," she added quickly. She lowered her eyes. "I'm here for you. That guy doesn't mean anything to me."

Christopher felt the muscles in his face relax. It was impossible to resist Aisha when she was this close, this beautiful, and speaking this sweetly. "Really?" he asked, leaning toward her.

"Yes, really," Aisha said, kissing him on the cheek. "I'll stop seeing him. I promise. It's as good as over."

"Oh, come on, Zo," Lucas Cabral said imploringly. "What's the big deal?"

"The big deal?" Zoey Passmore spat the words out in disgust and looked at her boyfriend through narrowed eyes. He had a guileless expression on his face, the moonlight reflecting off his wide, innocent-seeming eyes. "Lucas, you read my diary!" she shouted over the sound of crashing waves. "*After* you specifically promised not to." She flung her barn jacket over her shoulder and started walking quickly along the shore toward home.

"I said I was sorry," he said, trying to keep up with her.

She kept on walking, the sand crunching beneath her navy blue Converse sneakers. She and Nina had composed a fake diary entry about a rendezvous between Zoey and her so-called secret lover, Antonio, in order to test whether or not Lucas would peek into Zoey's diary. It had seemed like a good idea at the time, but then Zoey had been hoping that Lucas would pass the test. She hadn't planned what to do if he failed. Miserably.

"Come on, Zo. Talk to me," he begged.

Already Zoey felt herself softening, just as she always did when he started to sound desperate. But she didn't turn around. He'd really done it this time, and it was going to take a lot more than a "sorry" for her to forgive him.

"Please, Zoey," he said, catching up to her and grabbing her hand. He spun her around and made her face him. "Let's talk about it."

Zoey sighed heavily. The last thing she wanted was to be anywhere near him, but if she didn't give in, he would probably follow her all the way home.

"Just give me a chance to explain," he pleaded.

"Five—no, *two* minutes," she said, glancing down at her wristwatch. "You have exactly two minutes."

"Okay." He took a deep breath. "I'm sorry I looked at your diary. I won't do it again."

Zoey rolled her eyes.

"I just wanted to make sure, you know?" He looked at her hopefully, but then shook his head when he was met by a cold stare. "I mean, ever since the thing you had with Aaron, I've never been quite sure about where I stand with you."

"So you decided to sneak a peek at my most private thoughts," Zoey said, cocking her head and crossing her arms in front of her. "You couldn't have just asked. That would have been too easy—like asking for directions when you're lost or something."

Lucas let the remark pass. "And then when you got accepted to Berkeley, you decided to go there—*alone*—instead of to the University of Maine with me. . . ." He paused. "I don't know," he said quietly. "What's going to happen to us, Zo?"

It was a question Zoey had asked herself many times. But she was not yet ready to discuss it with Lucas. First there were some other issues that they needed to clear up once and for all. "In other words, you don't trust me," she said plainly. "So you've resorted to snooping and spying on me."

"No. That's not it," he protested. "I—"

"Admit it, Lucas. You don't trust me. I mean, if you

were ready to believe that I'd hooked up with some cheeseball named Antonio, obviously you'd believe just about anything."

"Okay, okay," he said, holding up his hands in surrender. "I thought it seemed corny, but I wasn't thinking very clearly. But, jeez, Zo, how can you blame me? After you cheated on me with that scumbag Mendel—"

"Oh, and you're the picture of innocence?" she said sarcastically. "I have one word for you, Lucas. Claire."

A pained look came over Lucas's face. "That was a mistake."

"Yeah, and I dealt with it," Zoey said stoutly, "without resorting to low-life behavior, like reading someone's private diary."

Lucas suddenly laughed contemptuously. "Yeah, right," he said. "You trusted me *completely* after that thing with Claire. That's why you were so convinced I was going behind your back with Lara—and then Kate!"

"That's different," Zoey said without much conviction.

"No, it's not," Lucas said, his voice rising. "You want to talk about trust?" He paused, moving his head slowly up and down. "Then let's talk about how *you* trust *me*."

Zoey sank down onto the sand. She had to admit he had a point. "Okay," she said. "You're right. Maybe we *both* need to learn how to trust each other more."

Lucas sat down next to her and scooped up a handful of sand. "Maybe."

They were both silent for a while. Zoey looked up at the sky and noticed that there was a perfect ring of light encircling the quarter moon. "We have no choice, really," she said. "Soon we'll be so far apart, it'll be impossible for us to spy on each other."

Lucas nodded.

"I guess we're going to *have* to trust each other." She looked at him, trying to read his expression, but his face was hidden in shadow. "We might as well start now."

"Truce, then?" he said, letting another handful of sand sift through his fingers.

"Yeah, okay," Zoey said. "Truce."

"You forgive me for reading your diary?" he asked.

"No," she said stubbornly. "And if I catch you looking through my things one more time, Lucas, I swear I'll never speak to you again."

Lucas held out his hand, and Zoey shook it. Then, in one swift motion, he pulled her onto his lap and started planting kisses all over her face and neck.

"Stop, Lucas," she said. "I'm still mad at you."

He stopped, and his dark eyes met hers. Zoey held her breath as the space between them narrowed inch by inch. She felt his lips brush against hers, and an instant later he was kissing her passionately.

Zoey

Where do I see myself in ten years? Tough question. I mean, let's face it—none of us really knows where we'll be in the future, particularly those of us who haven't even decided what to major in yet. But if I had to imagine, I guess I'd be

#1. thrilled about my recent engagement to a loyal, devoted, and trustworthy man (I hope it turns out to be Lucas)

#2. fighting off literary agents who want to represent me

#3. living with Nina in a sunny two-bedroom apartment with a cat named Ella and a spectacular view of the Golden Gate Bridge

#4. writing TV scripts for the soaps while working on my first novel

#5. the proud owner of a cute blue convertible (maybe a Volkswagen Cabriolet)

#6. tan all year round, with blond highlights in my hair

In ten years I'll be almost twenty-eight, which is almost thirty, which I hope means I won't still be dealing with stupid problems, like whether or not someone read my diary. Not that that's not a serious issue, because it definitely is. But it does seem small in the grand scheme of things . . . sort of disconnected from the real world somehow. I'll probably have bigger things to worry about when I'm nearly thirty.

11

Like getting my car insured, or whether I should marry the loyal, devoted guy or not, or whether to go with this agent or that one.

I wonder if Lucas and I will still be together. Will he still kiss me in the same heart-stopping way? Will we still be in love, or will we have grown apart? Will he be with someone else?

I just had a horrible thought. What if in ten years Lucas has a beer belly and has lost most of his hair?

Two

Benjamin Passmore felt the mattress move as Kate Levin abruptly stood up, gasping from shock.

"Oh, my God," she said. "I'm so sorry—and *so* embarrassed."

"Uh, well . . . ," he mumbled, trying to think of something to say. "I'm a little embarrassed, too, if it makes you feel any better."

Almost without even saying hello, Kate had given him an amazingly intimate kiss and told him that she was in love with him. It turned out she had mistakenly thought he was the one who'd come to help her after she'd accidentally been knocked unconscious in a fistfight between Aaron and Lucas some time earlier.

He would have stopped her if he had seen it coming, but, Benjamin thought ruefully, being blind meant he *hadn't* been able to see it coming. That kind of vulnerability just served as a reminder of at least a hundred other situations in which he found himself helpless compared to sighted people.

He could hear Kate pacing around the room. "But if it wasn't you," she said, finally perching on the edge of Benjamin's bed, "who was it?"

For a totally deluded love maniac, she certainly knows how to focus, Benjamin thought. He tried to remember the events of that evening just over two months before. He'd been pretty low because the experimental surgery he had hoped would allow him to see again had failed, and the disappointment was overwhelming. Zoey, his well-meaning but perhaps misguided sister, had decided a surprise birthday party would cure him of his depression. Benjamin had certainly been surprised, but *not* in a happy way, and the party had pretty much gone downhill from there. Aaron had arrived uninvited and had begun harassing Claire. Then Lucas had gotten involved, and in the end Kate had wound up in the wrong place and taken a punch in the face.

Benjamin struggled to remember the sounds from that night, but all that came back to him was the sound of Aaron and Lucas screaming at each other. After a moment he gave up. "Can't remember," he said.

"Are you sure?" Kate said, desperation creeping into her voice. "Are you absolutely sure you didn't see who carried me out?"

"Kate," Benjamin said in a monotone, "I'm blind. Of course I didn't *see* who carried you out."

"Oh," Kate said in a small voice. "I'm sorry."

As soon as he heard her tone, though, he wished he hadn't made that remark. Even though Kate was pissing him off with bizarre questions she shouldn't even be asking a sighted person, he didn't want to be rude to her.

"Okay," she said softly. "I won't bother—"

"It was Jake," he suddenly said with absolute certainty. Now he remembered Jake's voice shouting over the fray. Jake had been the one who had yelled, "Give her some air!"

"Jake!" Kate exclaimed. "Jake McRoyan?"

"Yes, Jake," Benjamin repeated blandly.

There was a brief pause.

"I . . . kind of blew him off last night," Kate finally said.

Benjamin sighed. He liked Kate, but he hadn't exactly asked to get involved in her love life.

Kate seemed to sense his impatience. "I'm sorry about this mixup," she said, getting up to go. "You probably think I'm totally insane."

"Don't worry." Benjamin rose and walked her to the door. "Let's just forget about it."

Kate took his hand. "Thanks," she said softly.

After she left, Benjamin lay down on his bed and replayed the final movement of the opera he had been listening to before Kate arrived. The encounter with her had been pretty strange, and he felt restless—as if he was suddenly aware of a huge void in the center of his life.

He had felt nothing from her kiss.

Absolutely nothing.

Claire threw on her robe and stormed out of the bathroom she shared with her younger sister, Nina. Twisting the belt around her waist, she stomped down the hallway to Nina's room and pounded on the door with a closed fist. "Dammit, Nina!" she yelled. "Open up."

It drove Claire nuts when Nina used up the last of her shampoo, conditioner, Q-Tips, or whatever, and Nina always did, of course—probably on purpose, just to annoy her. But this particular morning, a *Monday* morning, no less, was the wrong time to screw with Claire Geiger. Claire had been up half the night alternately reliving the moment Aaron had held her in his arms and chastising herself for actually enjoying physical contact with her dad's girlfriend's son, the cheating snake whom she had recently been in love with but now despised.

There was no response to Claire's pounding, but that wasn't unusual. Nina would do anything to catch an extra five minutes of sleep. Claire pushed her sister's door open and stepped inside. Nina's bed was slightly rumpled but still made. *Hmmm . . . maybe she finally got lucky and spent the night at Benjamin's,* Claire thought, chuckling at the unlikely scenario. *But she's probably just with Zoey.* She turned to leave, but a note taped to Nina's dresser mirror caught her eye.

Claire:

   Tell Dad I had to leave town for a while. I'm not sure where I'm going or when I'll be back. I took the emergency money from Dad's desk, so I'll be fine. Don't worry.
                    Nina

"Oh, man," Claire said, letting the note fall to the dresser top. "She's really lost it this time." She took a quick look into her dad's bedroom, then hurried down to the kitchen.

"Morning, Claire," Janelle, the Geigers' housekeeper, said cheerfully.

"Morning," Claire responded. "Do you know where my dad is?"

"Ayuh," Janelle said, using a Maine native's word for *yes*. "He had to leave early for a breakfast meeting." Janelle glanced at the clock. "Nina still sleeping? She'll be late for the ferry."

Claire nodded and didn't bother to explain that Nina had skipped town. If Janelle knew, she would probably fall to pieces. She'd been working for the Geigers since Claire's mother had passed away, five years before, and she was emotionally very attached to the girls. Janelle would eventually find out about the whole thing anyway. But at the moment Claire already had enough to deal with.

Claire walked across the spacious kitchen, the white tile floor cold against her bare feet. Her dad had mentioned a breakfast meeting to her . . . something about acquiring another piece of land on the island. She grabbed the phone from its cradle on the wall and punched in the number for her dad's cellular phone. It rang ten times with no answer.

"Great," Claire said, hanging up. Her dad must have turned off the phone. She sat down at the kitchen table and put her head in her hands. Something big must have happened with Benjamin for Nina to have taken off so suddenly. But what? She looked up at the wall clock. 7:32. Zoey and Benjamin were probably just leaving to catch the ferry, so it was no use calling them. And going to school was definitely out of the question. Claire had to somehow reach her father and let him know that his delinquent daughter was missing, and he probably wouldn't be in his office until nine o'clock.

Claire stood up and pulled the belt of her robe tighter. "I'm not going to school today, Janelle, so I'll be down for breakfast a little later." She turned and headed for the stairs before Janelle could ask any questions.

In her third-floor bedroom, Claire changed into a chenille pullover and a pair of old Levi's before climbing up the ladder that led to her private refuge, a widow's walk that had a spectacular view of the town, the island, the water, and the sky. It was her favorite place in the world. On a clear day like this, she could see the Chatham Island ferry landing, the lighthouse to the north, the cobblestone streets of North Harbor with all its quaint brick homes, and even the city of Weymouth on the mainland.

She'd spent many hours on this rooftop platform—writing in her diary, gazing up at the stars, noting the weather conditions. As an aspiring climatologist, Claire's specialty and passion was weather watching, and in the fall she was finally going to begin pursuing her dream at MIT. In four years Claire would earn her Bachelor of Science degree from the School of Earth, Atmospheric, and Planetary Sciences. But as thrilled as she was about going to MIT, Claire knew she would also miss so much about home: watching the clouds move across the overarching sky from her widow's walk, riding the ferry across the dark, calm depths of the sound, spending time with her father . . . even Nina. She would even miss her annoying, borderline twisted sister, at least in a weird sort of way.

A chill breeze blew right through her pullover, raising goose bumps on her arms. Without checking the thermometer, Claire could tell it was about fifty-five degrees. The sun had already burned through the thick fog that had settled in over the night, leaving a cloudless blue sky and excellent visibility.

Claire looked out across the water toward the mainland, trying to imagine her vulnerable sister making her way along the coast. She wondered if Nina was all right.

Zoey dropped her fork and urgently sucked down several mouthfuls of diet Coke to get rid of the taste in her mouth. "Ack. Gross," she said, sticking out her tongue.

"I kind of like it," Aisha said contentedly. "It's the only thing on the menu that's got any taste to it."

"Well, here you go," Zoey said, pushing her lunch tray across the table to Aisha. "Knock yourself out."

Aisha happily picked at the remainders of Zoey's sloppy joe while Zoey watched in disgust. Nina and Claire usually had lunch with them, too, but for some reason neither one had come to school that day. "Honestly, Eesh, I can't believe you're eating that stuff," she said. "I think you might have damaged your taste buds while making out with Christopher last night . . . or maybe it was *David* who did the damage," she added, laughing.

"Ha, ha," Aisha said, unamused. "They're going to just *love* your sophisticated sense of humor in California."

Zoey leaned across the table and smirked. "So, have you decided how you're going to dump David?" she asked. On the ferry ride to school that morning, Aisha had told Zoey all about the night before, adding the declaration that she was going to end it with David. Aisha had sounded so sure, but Zoey knew she wouldn't be able to give him up that easily.

Aisha frowned. "No. I haven't figured that out yet."

"Eesh," Zoey said seriously, "you don't have to

break up with David because of Christopher, you know. Just because he came back, that doesn't mean you owe him anything."

"But he came back to be with me," Aisha said plaintively. "And I love him, Zo. You know that."

Zoey nodded. She knew that Aisha did love Christopher—so much so that she had nearly gotten engaged to him just before he left the island to join the army. But Zoey also knew that Aisha had grown to care deeply for David. It had taken months for Aisha to admit that she was attracted to him, and the fact that he had been her main rival for the Westinghouse scholarship didn't help matters, but in the end she'd fallen for him anyway.

"I just don't know how I'm going to break it to David," Aisha went on, her forehead creased with worry. "And I definitely can't do it before Saturday. He's so excited about the prom. He's going to pick me up in Weymouth in a limo, and we're going to have dinner at Le Souffle."

Zoey winced. *Poor David.* "So you'll do it after prom weekend is over?"

"I guess," Aisha said with a sigh.

Zoey scratched her temple in thought. "Look. Why don't you do this?" she offered helpfully. "Just wait until next week before you do anything. Go to the prom with David, see how it goes with Christopher, and if you still want to break up with David by, say, Monday, then . . . well, it's over."

Frowning, Aisha slowly nodded. "That makes sense."

"Lucas and I are going to have dinner out before the prom, too," Zoey said in an attempt to change the topic and distract Aisha. "We're going to Seasons."

"Really?" Aisha said, looking at Zoey. "They're

having a special buffet for all the prom guests, right?"

"Yup," Zoey said, scooping up a spoonful of cherry-flavored Jell-O.

"I wanted to go there, too," Aisha said, "but David had something else in mind." She bit her lower lip. "Something more romantic."

Zoey sighed inwardly. Everything seemed to make Aisha think about David. "Have you decided which dress you're going back for?"

"The red one," Aisha said matter-of-factly. "The store is hemming it for me. My mom and I are picking it up after school tomorrow."

"Great," Zoey said. "Then you can wear the strappy black sandals, huh?"

Aisha nodded distractedly.

"You know, Nina's still hoping Benjamin will take her to the prom," Zoey said, hoping that getting away from the subject of the prom would force Aisha to think about something else. "But it really doesn't look like he's going to change his mind."

Aisha didn't respond. She was staring off into space.

"I really feel bad for her," Zoey continued. "I mean, I just feel like shaking him. He's been so out of it, don't you think?"

"Mmm-hmmm."

"And Claire doesn't want to go, either," Zoey said. "I think she thinks she's above going to proms or something." She paused. It was hard to carry on a conversation by yourself. "But we're going to have a blast, aren't we?"

"Sure."

Zoey reached over and tapped Aisha on the back of her hand. "Come on, Eesh. It'll be so much fun."

"I know," Aisha said, finally making eye contact. "I just wish Christopher could come, too." Aisha looked like she was about to cry. "Christopher and I have shared so much. I should be going with Christopher."

"But Eesh," Zoey pointed out gently, "you've already said yes to David. You can't back out now."

Aisha shook her head. "It's not right, Zo," she said decisively. "I think I should break up with David *before* the prom—and then I can go with the person I really want to go with: Christopher."

Zoey considered this for a moment. "It'll break David's heart," she said.

"But would it be fair if I went with him even though I really want to be with Christopher?" Aisha's voice was rising with emotion. "Would it be fair if I ride around in the limo with him all night, go out for this romantic dinner, go to the prom with him, and *then* dump him?"

Zoey lowered her eyes and shook her head. No, it wouldn't be fair.

Poor David.

Three

Nina stared at a spot of dried ketchup on the linoleum tabletop, images of Benjamin kissing Kate running through her mind for the hundredth time. She squeezed her eyes shut, willing the images to disappear. Her eyes felt tired and swollen from crying. She'd hardly had any sleep, and she felt as if she'd shriveled up and aged thirty years in the course of one long night.

It was all a blurry nightmare to her now. After seeing Kate's mouth on Benjamin's, her fingers buried in his dark hair, all Nina could think of was getting as far away as possible. After taking the last ferry to Weymouth the night before, she'd sat on a bench outside the station for hours, wishing she had enough money to make it to California. Then she'd gone to the bus station and boarded the first bus that was leaving. The next thing she knew, she was waking up on a hard bench in the Portland bus station, a smelly old man spitting up phlegm just two feet away. Normally Nina would have grabbed her duffel and run for the door, but that morning nothing fazed her—not even the filthy, urine-scented bathroom she'd been forced to wash up in. Now that she'd *really* lost Benjamin, nothing mattered. She wouldn't even have minded wearing Laura Ashley dresses every day for the rest of her life.

". . . you'd like, miss?"

Nina slowly shifted her gaze to a rosy-cheeked waitress, who was smiling down at her pleasantly. "Huh?"

"I said, do you know what you'd like?"

Nina shook her head. "No. I mean, yes. A cup of coffee." She brought her focus back to the spot of ketchup as the waitress nodded and left.

How could she have been so stupid? How could she have actually believed that the old Benjamin, the one who loved her more than anything in the world, would eventually come back to her? Her eyes began to sting, and the ketchup stain went out of focus. Nina had truly believed that Benjamin had never stopped loving her, that he just needed time and space to get over the disappointment of the failed surgery.

How could she have been so wrong? Nina asked herself. And now what was she going to do? Blinking rapidly in an effort to keep the tears from coming, Nina fished around in her pockets for her Lucky Strikes. She had no idea where she was going next. All she knew was that she couldn't bear to be on Chatham Island, where everyone knew how pitiful she was.

"Here you go, miss," the waitress said, putting a cracked white mug down in front of her. "Would you like anything else?"

Nina popped a cigarette in the corner of her mouth and shook her head.

The waitress frowned. "I'm sorry, miss," she said politely. "This is the nonsmoking section."

"Don't worry," Nina said, taking a deep drag off her unlit cigarette. "I never light them."

The waitress looked at her uncertainly. "Oh . . . well, I guess it's okay, then."

Nina watched the waitress make her way down the aisle, pouring coffee for various customers. There was something really annoying about the way her pink skirt kept flouncing around every time she took a step.

Nina took a sip of the black coffee. It was watery and almost soapy-tasting, but its warmth felt good in her empty stomach. Maybe she was overreacting, she thought. It wouldn't be the first time. Not too long before, she'd been convinced that Benjamin was fooling around with Aisha behind her back, but it had turned out Aisha was just secretly helping him surf the Net for information about the surgery for reversing blindness. She put her cigarette back in her mouth and inhaled thoughtfully. A tiny bit of hope flickered in the back of her mind as she toyed with the possibility that Benjamin really did love her and that she'd jumped to the wrong conclusion once again. But then the images came flooding back: Kate's long red hair brushing against his black shirt, his open palm pressed against her back, the glint of lamplight reflecting off his Ray-Bans, Kate's eyes shut in pleasure . . . the picture was so hideously clear and vivid, Nina could still smell the scent of Kate's skin lotion.

No, there was definitely no mistake this time. This time Nina had seen it with her own eyes. Benjamin had moved on without her. When he'd told her that he didn't love her anymore, he'd been telling her nothing but the truth.

Nina

In ten years? I'll probably be sitting in a jail cell, doing time for the violent murder of Kate Levin and muttering to myself about the injustice of it all. "It was a crime of passion. Haven't you ever been in love? She deserved it!" I'll cry out to anyone who happens to walk by my cell.

And I'll probably be suffering from early menopause, too. Hot and cold flashes, sudden mood swings, bouts of irrational behavior. So then they'll send me to the asylum, where they'll shoot me up with large doses of Valium and phenobarbital and morphine. My friends won't want to have anything to do with me, and Sarah will convince my father that it's best just to pretend I was never born. Claire will probably stop by once in a while with her gorgeous husband and two perfect kids, but I'll pretend not to recognize them.

And what about Benjamin? He won't even know that I'm in the asylum because no one will want to break the news to him. They'll probably tell him that I died in jail.

Four

"Hi, Janelle," Zoey said when the housekeeper opened the door. "Is Nina in?"

"No," she said nervously, "she's . . . she's . . . oh, I'd better let Claire tell you." She opened the door wider and gestured for Zoey and Lucas to come in.

Zoey gave Lucas a puzzled look as they stepped into the Geigers' elegant foyer and dropped their backpacks on the floor. Zoey had eventually gotten so worried about why Nina and Claire hadn't come to school that she'd insisted they go to the Geigers' straight from the ferry.

Janelle didn't seem to be her usual cheerful self, Zoey noted. She looked almost as if she'd been crying. What was going on? Was one of the family really sick or something? "Thanks," Zoey said to Janelle, heading for the stairs. "We'll go up and find her."

From the third-floor landing, Zoey could hear Claire tapping away at her computer. Her bedroom door was open, and Zoey peered in. "Hi," she said. "We were just wondering why you guys skipped school today. Is someone sick or something?"

Claire swiveled around in her chair. She was sitting in the lotus position. Secured only by a pencil, her long, jet-black hair was swept up in an elegant French twist. "No," she said, looking directly at Zoey with a grim expression. "Nina's run away."

"What do you mean, she's run away?" Zoey said, taking a step over the threshold, Lucas right behind her.

Claire reached into her desk drawer and pulled out a piece of paper. "She took off last night. Here—look at this if you want."

Zoey crossed the room and took the paper from Claire's outstretched hand. Lucas read over her shoulder as Zoey quickly scanned the note.

"Man," he said, looking at Claire in disbelief. "What happened?"

"I was kind of hoping *you'd* enlighten me," Claire said to Zoey expectantly.

Zoey sank down on Claire's bed and read the note one more time. *Don't worry,* it said. But already Zoey was worried. Why would Nina do this? And why hadn't she come and talked to Zoey first? Zoey shook her head slowly and swallowed. "I—I don't know," she said, feeling like a complete and total failure. Some best friend she was. "I don't know."

"Have you heard anything from her yet?" Lucas asked with concern.

Claire shook her head. "Nothing."

"Do you have any idea where she might have gone?" he said.

"Well, my dad and I spent the day making phone calls to people she might have run to," Claire said, sighing. "And I was just about to call you to find out if you knew anything . . . but so far we've drawn a total blank."

Lucas sat on the bed next to Zoey and put his arm around her shoulders. She didn't know what to think. This had come out of left field. She knew that Nina had been depressed about Benjamin lately, but she had somehow allowed herself to forget. Instead, she'd leaned on Nina—for comic relief, for warmth and comfort—as she always did. If only Nina had come to her. If only Nina had trusted her. Zoey should have known that something was bothering Nina. And she should have found a way to help her. That was what best friends were for.

Claire broke abruptly into Zoey's thoughts. "Nina was over at your house last night, wasn't she?"

Zoey looked at Claire and suddenly burst into tears. She buried her face in Lucas's shoulder, ashamed that she had spent hours with Nina the night before and not even known how upset she was. She had been too preoccupied with her own problems to even ask Nina how she was doing. Maybe Nina would have told her what was wrong if she'd given her a chance. But instead all Zoey had done was talk about how she was setting Lucas up and how he had better not show up at the beach. Zoey was racked with guilt. She had acted so selfishly.

Lucas stroked Zoey's hair and rocked her gently. "Shhh," he said softly. "She'll be fine, Zo. Don't worry."

Claire handed Zoey a box of tissues, and Zoey took one and blew her nose. "Yes," she finally said, still sobbing. "She had dinner at my house." She took a deep breath, trying to steady her quavering voice. "But she didn't tell me anything."

"What about Benjamin?" Claire persisted. "Was he home? Do you think they might have had a fight or something?"

Zoey nodded, frowning. "I think he was in his room when Nina left. So maybe," she said, shrugging. "I don't know."

Claire pulled the pencil out of her hair and combed her fingers through her shiny black mane. She stuck the pencil in her mouth and chewed on it thoughtfully.

"It's all my fault," Zoey said miserably. "Because . . . because I knew she was still hurting about Benjamin, but I was getting sick of hearing about it all the time . . . so like a week ago I told her to forget about him and move on." A fresh wave of sobs burst from her, and she pulled another tissue from the box. "I can't believe I said that," she said, choking on her tears.

"Hey," Lucas said, smoothing her hair away from her wet face. "It's not your fault."

"But it *is*," Zoey said. She felt a sob rising in her chest. "It *is* my fault."

"And Benjamin hasn't said anything to you?" Claire asked.

Zoey shook her head.

In response to Claire's questioning look, Lucas merely shrugged. "I haven't spoken to him all day," he said.

"Did he seem distracted," Claire said, leaning forward over her folded legs, "or weird or anything?"

"Just like he always is," Zoey said.

"Well." Claire unfolded her legs and stood up from her desk chair. "I think we should go see what Benjamin has to say for himself."

Five

Benjamin slipped under the satin sheets, relishing their cool smoothness against his skin. Like many of his clothes and other furnishings, he had chosen the sheets for tactile stimulation. He had just had another grueling day at school, especially with Mrs. Homes, the guidance counselor, on his back about getting the credits he needed to graduate. With less than a month left of school, Benjamin was really making a push to catch up on all the work he had blown off while he recovered both physically and emotionally from his surgery. He had an extra-credit paper to write by the next day, but all he wanted to do was take a nap.

There was a knock at his door. Zoey. Even in his half-asleep state, Benjamin could recognize her knock.

"What?" he cried irritably. "I'm trying to sleep."

"Sorry," Zoey said through the door. "It's important."

He sat up in bed and put on his Ray-Bans, thoroughly annoyed. "Come in."

"Claire and Lucas are with me, too," Zoey said, closing the door.

Benjamin groaned. This had better not be another one of those concerned-friend talks he'd been constantly subjected to since his surgery.

"What is it?" he said shortly.

Zoey sat at the foot of his bed. "Um," she said, clearing her throat. "We have some awful news, Benjamin." She paused, and Benjamin made himself be patient. "Nina," she said, faltering, "Nina's . . ."

"Nina's what, Zoey?" Benjamin said, pushing the bedsheets off him.

"Nina's run away," Claire said flatly.

You could always count on Claire to tell it like it was. From the direction of her voice, Benjamin knew she was sitting on the floor by his rolltop desk. "What do you mean, she's run away?" Benjamin asked. He felt momentarily light-headed, as if he'd sat up too quickly.

"She took off last night," Claire said.

Benjamin remained silent, struggling to hide his shock.

"We were wondering if she said anything to you first," Claire continued.

Benjamin swallowed. *Where would she go? How is she taking care of herself?*

"Benjamin?" Claire said. "Do you know what happened?"

Benjamin shook his head. "I didn't really talk to her last night."

"Did you notice anything about her?" Lucas asked. "We thought maybe—"

Benjamin aimed his dark glasses in the general direction of Lucas's voice. He, too, seemed to be sitting on the floor. "No, I didn't notice anything strange. And she definitely didn't say anything to me," he responded.

He felt Zoey slide over closer to him. "You guys didn't have another fight, did you?" she asked cautiously.

Benjamin didn't like the implications of the question. Zoey seemed to be blaming him. "No," he said, his shock turning into anger. "I've hardly said two words to her in the last several days."

"Okay, then," Claire said, getting up to go. "You'll call me if you hear from her?"

Benjamin nodded. "Of course."

Benjamin slipped back under the covers and listened as the three trooped out of his room. Why would she have run away? Was it his fault?

Everyone seemed to be implying that. But it wasn't his fault he no longer felt the same way about her. And it wasn't her fault, either. Benjamin had changed since his surgery, and he wished everyone would just accept it. They all expected him to go back to being Benjamin the blind wonder. The one who was perpetually in denial about being blind.

He closed his eyes and tried to sleep, but it was useless. He was too agitated about the whole thing with Nina. Everyone was going to blame him—for breaking up with her, for not loving her anymore, for making her life miserable. He slammed his palms against his mattress. It wasn't his fault! He'd just done what he had to do.

He flipped over onto his stomach and hugged his pillow against his chest. It wasn't his fault that she couldn't handle the breakup. He'd tried to avoid breaking up with her, but every day he'd grown more and more distant, and being with him seemed to hurt her even more.

"What was I supposed to do?" he asked himself out loud.

Everything he did and said seemed to hurt her. Nina was so tough on the outside, with her Lucky Strikes and her sharp tongue. She could easily provoke a fight with someone who didn't know her. But inside, she was incredibly fragile.

Benjamin sighed. Not many people realized how vulnerable and naive she really was. Maybe not even Nina.

If you had asked me that question
last year—before January fifth, to be
precise, which was the day my life was
supposed to change back to normal—I
would have answered very differently.
Back then I had been blind for seven
years, and though it was a condition I
was used to, I guess I never really
believed that I would spend the rest of
my life in total darkness. Holding out
that hope was my way of coping with
the blindness, I suppose.

So I might have dared to say that in
ten years I would be a seeing person.
My television watching wouldn't be rel-
egated to talk shows. My wardrobe
would include some colored pieces, not
just black and white. I would be able to
read on my own. I would be able to go
anywhere by myself without fearing
for my life. And maybe I would love
myself enough to be able to love someone else.

But January fifth has long since
come and gone, and I no longer have
any false hopes. I will be blind for the
rest of my life. So when you ask me
where I see myself ten years from

now, I don't really even have to think about it. In ten years I will still be blind, living life in the same limited way. The only difference is, I will be older and more educated and more comfortable with the blackness that surrounds me.

Six

c) Rellena los espacios con en el tiempo pasado:

Mi abuelo (ser) _era_ un hombre alto, fuerte y de grandes convicciones. Su aspecto se (hacer) _____ menos imponente cuando (actuar) _____ pues (ser) _____ amable y cortés y siempre (gustarle) _____ complacer a la gente que le (rodear) _____.

"Hacer. Hacer. Hacer," Jake repeated over and over. *How do you say that in the past tense?* He chewed on a hangnail, deep in concentration. *Could it be* hacía?

Oh, God, he was in so much trouble. How was he going to pass the final? This was just a stupid exercise. He basically knew what the words in the parentheses meant, but he had no idea what the rest of the sentence was all about, except that it had something to do with his grandfather. Was it *hizo?* Did that sound right?

Jake looked up from his textbook. He thought he heard a knock.

"Jake!" He heard a muffled voice calling him from outside the sliding glass doors that led from the patio to his bedroom. Then a knock.

Oh, no, he thought. *Lara. And she's probably*

toasted. Emborrachada. Lara McAvoy was Zoey and Benjamin's half sister. She and Jake used to have drinking binges together, which had been the basis of something like a relationship. But when Jake had suggested she join AA and sober up, she'd refused. He had avoided her ever since, but Lara couldn't seem to accept that it was over between them, and she was determined to get him back.

If he waited long enough, maybe she'd go away, he thought. But he realized he was just kidding himself. He knew Lara. She wasn't going anywhere—especially if she was drunk.

He closed his book on his pen, got up, and peered through the blinds. He wanted to know what state she was in before opening the door.

But it was Kate. She saw him looking at her, and she waved and smiled. He pulled the cord to open the blinds, then slid open the door. "Hi," he said, feeling a flutter in his stomach. Kate was the most beautiful woman he had ever laid eyes on. What was she doing at Jake's door?

"Hi," she said, stepping inside. She looked so happy to see him that it made Jake nervous. "I've been trying to track you down since last night," she said. "You're a busy person."

"Uh, yeah," he said, puzzled. "I work out and stuff." He pulled out his desk chair for her to sit on, then went back to his bed.

"I know you're probably surprised I'm here," she said, a huge grin on her face. "But I think you'll be happy when I tell you why."

Jake fluffed up his pillow and leaned against it. He couldn't believe that Kate, perfect Kate, was sitting in his bedroom. He suddenly noticed his big toe was sticking out of a hole in his sock, and he self-consciously tried to hide it by crossing his ankles. "Great," he said, for lack of anything better to say.

Kate leaned forward. "Remember when you asked me out, and I said I was involved with someone else?"

"Yes," Jake said. How could he forget? He had felt so rejected and utterly stupid. He and Kate had seemed to be hitting it off pretty well—they'd spent some time wandering around the shore, talking, while she snapped some pictures of him. So when he'd asked her out at a party after a baseball game, he really hadn't expected her to say no.

"Well," Kate went on, "I wasn't exactly *involved* with anyone. But I was looking for the person I wanted to be involved with."

Her words weren't making much sense to him, but he tried to concentrate. "Uh-huh," he said, trying to encourage her to go on.

"Are you with me so far?" she asked, cocking her head.

"Well, no. Not really."

"Okay. Let me explain," she said, her eyes sparkling excitedly. "Remember at the Passmores' when Lucas accidentally punched me and knocked me out?"

"Yeah." He couldn't forget that. There had been a lot of blood. And Jake hated the sight of blood.

"You carried me out to the foyer, right?" she said.

Jake nodded. Where was all this heading?

"Well," she said dreamily, "I think I started to fall in love with you at that moment. You were so sweet and so gentle. I felt like I was in a dream."

"Wait a minute," Jake said. This was really weird. He uncrossed his ankles and sat up. "You can't fall in love with someone when you're unconscious," he said, punctuating the statement by waving his hand in the air. "I mean, that's impossible. Right?"

Kate laughed. "I didn't exactly say I was in love with you," she explained. "I said I *started* to fall in love with the person who cradled me in his arms."

"Oh," Jake said, though he still didn't quite get it.

"And since then I've gotten to know you better," she said, "and I . . . I really like you."

A blush rose to her cheeks as she spoke, and Jake smiled in spite of his bewilderment. She was so beautiful. "So you, uh, came here to tell me that?"

Kate was grinning and nodding vigorously.

"Well . . . thanks," he said. "I guess."

"So maybe we can do something sometime," she said hopefully.

"Uh, sure," he said, feeling flattered and trapped at the same time. He wasn't yet sure how he felt about this bizarre turn of events. On the one hand, there was something special about Kate. On the other, he got the distinct feeling that she wasn't necessarily interested in *him,* Jake. She was in love with this fictional person from her dreams. Because if she had been interested in the real Jake, she wouldn't have turned him down when he asked her out before . . . would she?

"So what about tomorrow?" she suggested. "I need to pick up some art supplies from the mall. Maybe you can meet me there after school."

"Um . . . sure. Okay," he said uncertainly.

"Great." She leaped up. "Around four-fifteen in front of the Gap?"

He was about to say yes when he realized he had to go to an AA meeting right after school. "Actually, I won't be able to make it till around five-thirty," he said.

"That's okay," she said. "Five-thirty, then."

Jake gave her an awkward smile.

"Well, I don't want to cut in on your studying time," she said, glancing at the textbook on his bed. "And I've got a project due myself. So I'll see you tomorrow?" She took a step toward him.

"Yup," he said, scratching the back of his neck. "See you tomorrow."

Before he knew what was happening, Kate rose up on tiptoe and kissed him softly on the cheek. It was just a friendly kiss, but it sent a tingle through Jake's body, from head to toe. He knew that he was blushing.

"Bye," Kate said, waving as she slipped out the door.

Jake smiled—and kept on smiling as he sat on his bed and tried to go back to his studying. He touched his cheek. Kate was really nice, he thought. And gorgeous. But *definitely* a little strange.

Claire forced herself to swallow a forkful of scalloped potatoes. As much as she didn't feel like eating, she didn't want to hurt Janelle's feelings. After all, the housekeeper had spent all afternoon cooking.

"These potatoes are delicious, Janelle," Burke Geiger said halfheartedly as the housekeeper refilled his water glass.

"Oh, yes," Sarah Mendel added with a phony smile. "Just perfect. Well . . . maybe just a tiny bit too much cream." She indicated a pinch by pressing her thumb and forefinger together.

It was just like Sarah to diminish a compliment on Janelle's cooking. Sarah had always been slightly insecure about how well Janelle managed the Geiger household, Claire noted. But recently she'd been taking more little digs at Janelle than usual—and Claire suspected it had something to do with the recent tension between Sarah and her father. Tension for which Claire was directly responsible.

It came as no surprise to Claire that Sarah was feeling a little more insecure lately. It was exactly what Claire had planned. The week before, Sarah had found a love letter addressed to Claire's father from another woman, which instigated a huge fight. It was Claire who had actually written and mailed the letter, hoping that it would lead to their breakup, but after a tempestuous few days of nonstop fighting, Sarah and Claire's father had decided to postpone the wedding and give the relationship another chance, which meant Claire still had some work to do. Her mission was to stop her unsuspecting father from marrying the dwarflike woman who had spawned Aaron, and she wasn't going to quit until it was accomplished. She would rather die than have that vile pair as her stepmother and stepbrother.

Claire looked over at her father's plate. Like Claire, he'd hardly eaten a thing, and the scalloped-potatoes comment was probably just his attempt at normal conversation. Nina was obviously on everyone's mind; yet, oddly, no one was talking about her. In fact, no one was really even talking.

Finally Sarah broke the silence. "Burke, maybe we should ask Claire's opinion on what we were discussing earlier," she said, laying a miniature hand on top of his.

Claire's father considered the suggestion for a moment, then looked across the table at Claire. "Good idea," he said, smiling at Claire supportively. "Claire's got a good head on her shoulders."

This sounds interesting, Claire thought, laying down her fork.

"Claire," Sarah began, "your father and I were just talking about how to approach this problem we're having with Nina."

We're having. The phrase made Claire choke on the water she was drinking.

"I feel that with all that's been going on lately," she continued in her best Carol-Brady-in-a-crisis voice, "our engagement, wedding plans, and so on, your father and I haven't been spending much quality time with you girls."

Good going, Nina. Now the midget is going to spend quality time with us.

"So I think Nina might have been feeling a little neglected," Sarah said sagely, "especially since she hasn't been getting much attention from the Passmore boy, either."

Claire's father put his elbows on the table and clasped his hands together. "What exactly *did* happen between Benjamin and Nina?" he asked Claire.

"Let me finish, Burke," Sarah said, glancing sharply at Claire's father. "I think what Nina needs right now is a lot of love and attention."

Claire almost laughed. If Nina knew that coming home would mean more love and attention from Sarah, she'd definitely never come back.

"The fact that Nina ran away is an indication of that need," Sarah continued, "a cry for attention, so to speak."

This was absurd. But it did shed some light on Aaron's perversity. Claire shifted her eyes to her father. "So you think Nina ran away because you and Sarah have been too busy with your wedding to pay any attention to her?"

"No," he said. "It's not that simple."

"Well, of course that's why, Burke," Sarah said, shooting him an impatient look. "And I think we should find her and go after her," she added firmly, "to show her that we love her and that we care about her welfare more than anything."

"That's not necessarily the best thing to do in this case," Claire's father argued.

"Of course it is," Sarah insisted, delicately dabbing at the corners of her mouth with her napkin. "If we don't, she'll think we're too busy to even notice she's gone."

"Claire, what do you think?" her father said, not waiting for an answer. "I *don't* think we should go chasing her around the country. Nina's very independent," he said, looking at Claire for confirmation. "She'll resent us if we force her to come back when she's not ready."

Claire nodded. They didn't really care what she thought. This argument was between Sarah and her father, and though it was ostensibly about Nina, Claire detected an unmistakable undercurrent of other tension as well.

"She went away to think and work things out on her own," her father continued. "She's grappling with her very first heartbreak, which is never easy, and the fact that all her friends will be leaving for college soon doesn't make it any easier."

"Burke," Sarah said in a condescending tone, "I know what I'm talking about. I brought up Aaron practically on my own, and I know what these children need."

Aaron: the quintessential human being. Claire could barely stifle a laugh.

Claire's father sighed, frustrated. "All I'm saying is, she's going through a lot, and maybe you're right that we haven't been paying much attention to her, and maybe that's part of it, but going after her is not the solution. She needs this time to figure it out on her own." His voice was rising. "And she'll be back of her own volition when she's ready."

"Oh," Sarah said, disgusted, "you men always think you know everything, but you know *nothing,* especially when it comes to child rearing."

"Enough, Sarah," Claire's father said angrily. "I've

heard *enough*. She's *my* daughter, and I say we leave her alone."

Claire looked from one to the other. *Well, glad I could help.*

Sarah was just about to storm out of the room when the phone rang. All three rushed into the kitchen, but Janelle had already picked up the receiver. "It's Nina," she mouthed, looking at Claire's father. "Just a minute," she said aloud. "I'll get him."

Claire's father took the phone. "Nina, where are you? Are you all right?"

Claire rushed to the den and picked up the extension. "Hi, Nina!" she said. "How're you doing?"

"Jeez, I'm fine," Nina said. "I just wanted to get away for a while."

"Nina, why?" Claire's father asked, his voice on the verge of breaking. "What happened? Is it something we can help you with?"

"No, there's nothing you can do," Nina said. "Look, I'm not ready to talk about it, okay, Dad?"

"Okay. But honey, please tell me where you are."

"Somewhere safe, Dad. That's all you need to know."

"Is there a phone number there?"

"Dad!"

"Look, what if I promise not to come after you? Will you tell me?"

Nina sighed, sounding exasperated. "I gotta go."

"No, no, Nina. Don't go."

"Dad," Claire said plainly, "she's not going to tell us where she is."

"Oh, honey," Claire's father said. "Why don't you just come home?"

"I can't right now, Dad," Nina answered, her voice

trembling a tiny bit. "I just called to tell you that I'm okay."

"Well, when do you plan on coming back?"

"I don't know."

"All right," he said, more calmly. "But remember that we'll welcome you back anytime you're ready . . . do you have enough money?"

"No problem there," Nina said. "I took the emergency stash."

"I don't want you staying in rinky-dink places, you understand? Only safe places, big hotels. You can charge it all to me."

"Okay."

"Will you promise to call us every day?"

"I'll try."

"Nina, please be careful out there," Claire's father said imploringly. "Don't talk to strangers."

A recording came on the line. "Please deposit forty-five cents for the next three minutes. Please deposit—"

"Look, I have to go now. I don't have any more change."

"Give me your number, and we'll call you back," Claire's father said.

"No, I'd better go now."

"Okay, sweetheart. Call us again tomorrow."

Claire hung up and went back into the kitchen. Her father was sitting at the table, looking completely drained. "Claire," he said, looking up at her, "do you think I'm doing the right thing by not going after her?"

Sarah glared at him disdainfully. "You don't know *what* you're doing," she said before Claire had a chance to respond. Then she spun around and left the room.

A second later Claire's father got up to go after Sarah.

This is going to be easy, Claire thought. *This breakup might even happen on its own.*

Claire

I'll tell you where I won't be ten years from now. I <u>won't</u> be part of a family that includes Aaron and the munchkin, that's for sure.

But where do I see myself?

You know, it's amazing, but I can actually see myself ten years from now pretty clearly. I'll still be essentially the same person. Same face, same hair, private, kind of a loner. But in ten years I'll have my own money, a solid career, real independence, and an even stronger sense of self.

I see myself as goal-oriented and driven, and I imagine that I'll glean a lot of personal fulfillment from my

47

work, which I will undoubtedly love, since it'll have something to do with climatology or meteorology. And I don't mean that I'm going to end up chasing tornadoes, like the Helen Hunt character in Twister. Nor do I see myself as the weather girl on channel nine.

Will there be a man in my life ten years from now? That part I don't know. And, frankly, it doesn't really matter. I believe that the men will always be there as long as you know who you are and what you're doing.

Honor and Intimacy
By Zoey Passmore

~~Tina Geiger is my best fr~~

~~Tina Geiger, smart, funny, and my best friend~~

~~Tina Sniger, smart, funny, and my best friend, had a pretty good life at the age of sixteen.~~

~~Sixteen-year-old Tina Sniger was Zoey Passmore's best frie~~

Tina Sniger, pretty, clever, and funny, had lived nearly seventeen years in the world. Though her mother had died when she was only eleven, her existence was generally blessed, with a wealthy and indulgent father and a secure and happy life on Chamden, a beautiful island off the coast of England.

She was a very pretty girl, although she herself didn't think so, and was therefore never boastful. She had soft gray eyes and a general look of sweetness in spite of her best efforts to seem less than amiable. She dressed in a somewhat unconventional manner, and she was often more outspoken and bold than was socially appreciated. Nevertheless, Tina enjoyed uncommon popularity among good society, and no one spoke of her without goodwill.

Indeed, the only real evil of Tina's situation was that she had entrusted her friendship to an unworthy and inferior young woman, Chloe Trashbore, who was rather coarse and unfit to be her intimate.

Tina's beau, Benny Tessmore, was a handsome and intelligent young man with a warm heart and a witty disposition. Their connection was generally regarded as quite suitable, and it produced great happiness for many fortnights. It was known to all that Tina and Benny were very much in love, and that they each admired the other to the utmost degree.

But, alas, Benny suffered a grave and serious malady, which left him afflicted by blindness, and caused alarm in the hearts of all his intimates, most especially Tina, who called on him constantly, and earnestly tried to nurse him back to health. She attempted to disperse his ill humor with wit and flattery, and to raise his spirits with an outpouring of all her love, but her efforts were in vain: He was comfortless.

At first Benny seemed much gratified by the kind care of such a fair lady, but soon he grew restless in her company, and brought their alliance to an end. This caused Tina much pain and humiliation, and she suffered as she never had before in all her sixteen years.

Chloe stood by and watched as Tina's tears fell abundantly, and for a time, genuinely concerned for her friend's welfare, she tried to console her with all her understanding. Chloe could not but pity poor Tina, for her wounds seemed to result

from real feeling for Benny,
who had seemed so worthy
of her affection.

But after days and days
of listening to Tina's
lamentations, Chloe grew
weary and began to con-
sider all that had passed
as quite unworthy of being
dwelt upon.

"You need not think
about this unfortunate situation

Seven

With a backpack that felt like it weighed a ton, Aisha lumbered down the gangplank after the ferry docked at the Chatham Island terminal. *Why don't they split textbooks into multiple volumes so that students like me don't have to spend the rest of their lives permanently stooped?* she wondered. Her six-hundred-page physics textbook was doing the most damage, she knew. But since she had a big physics test the next day, she'd had no choice but to lug it after school to the Weymouth library, where she'd been studying until the library was nearly ready to close. Now it was 9:25, and she had promised Christopher that she'd spend some time with him before heading back to Gray House.

"Don't scream and I won't hurt you," said a familiar voice.

Aisha spun around and saw Christopher standing on the pier a few feet away. Grinning widely, he took the backpack from her and swept her into his arms. "I couldn't wait to see you," he said, kissing her warmly on the lips.

Aisha laughed, her weariness slipping away almost instantly. "You're supposed to be waiting for me in there," she said, pointing to the Redwood Inn on Exchange Street.

"I was," he said, shrugging, "but you were taking too long."

Aisha wrapped an arm around his waist and playfully rubbed his washboard stomach with her free hand. "Oh, it's so good to have you home," she said as they approached the inn. "And I'm so sorry I couldn't come home right after school."

"Hey, it's precisely that kind of discipline that gets people into Princeton," he said, winking at her. "And besides, you've already apologized."

They walked through the quaint inn's small lobby to get to the six-table coffee shop at the back.

After they had sat down and placed their orders, Christopher gave Aisha the rundown of his first day of job hunting. He had hit every major business on the island, primarily inns and a couple of restaurants, but so far, nothing. "But it's only my first day," he said. "I'm sure I'll find something soon."

Throughout the job-search discussion, Christopher had remained calm, but suddenly he leaned forward and his eyes grew hard. "Did you break up with that guy?" he asked in a low voice. For a moment Aisha was speechless. She hadn't, of course. In fact, she'd avoided David all day.

"Um, no," she said, taken aback. "Not today. But tomorrow . . ." She faltered.

"Did you see him today?" Christopher demanded.

Just then the waitress arrived, and Aisha waited until she had set down Christopher's soda and Aisha's tea and gone back behind the counter.

"No," Aisha finally said. "I have calculus with him, but we didn't really have a chance to talk or . . ." She let her voice trail off.

"Are you gonna see him tomorrow?" he demanded,

taking a sip of his Sprite and replacing the glass carefully on the table in front of him.

Aisha frantically searched through her mind for an excuse. There was always the truth, of course. That she intended to go to the prom with David and break up with him afterward. But obviously that would never go over. Why did Christopher have to put her through this? She'd already told him that she would break up with David. *When* she did it was inconsequential. As long as it was before the weekend, anyway. "I don't know," she answered. "Maybe."

"Eesh," he said, gazing directly into her eyes. "When are you going to do it?"

She looked at him blankly. She didn't know exactly when. When the opportunity arose, she supposed. "It?" she asked. *When in doubt, stall,* she thought.

"Yeah, Eesh. When are you going to inform him that you already have a boyfriend and—surprise, surprise—it's not him?"

Aisha twisted the string of the tea bag around her finger. "Well, uh, Wednesday, I guess," she mumbled. "I think I can do it on Wednesday, because by then I'll be done with the physics test and the, uh, bio lab."

Christopher nodded, apparently satisfied, but Aisha could feel the tension in the air. They needed a change of subject. And now would be a good time for it. "Hey," she said, thinking of the perfect topic, "the senior prom's this Saturday, and I was thinking that maybe—if you want to—we could go together." She untwisted the string wrapped around her finger, letting the blood flow back into her fingertip.

"That sounds great," he said. He looked at her brightly, and his mouth broke into a giant grin. "I never got to go to my own prom, not that it was anything big. But I'd love to."

"I'll get the tickets," she said. "It'll be like my homecoming present to you." The move had worked: Christopher was happy again. But it also meant that Aisha definitely had to break up with David before the prom. Which as far as Aisha was concerned was great, because finally the time for waffling was over. There was no going back. This time on Wednesday David Barnes would be history.

Eight

"I'm so psyched," Kate said to Jake as she dropped her wallet into her purse. "They had everything I needed. That *never* happens."

Jake took the package from the cashier. "Maybe you just need to take me shopping more often," he said, smiling.

"Is that a promise?" Kate asked.

"Yup, as long as you promise to come to more of my games."

Kate hooked her arm in his, and they went out into the mall. "So, are you hungry?" she asked. "Because I'm starving."

"Yeah, I could eat," Jake said. "Food court?"

Kate nodded, a huge grin on her face. After having searched for so long, she couldn't believe she was finally with the guy who had saved her. Everything was working out so perfectly.

They walked toward the other end of the mall, where the food court was. On their way they passed Michaela, Kate's favorite boutique.

"Oh," she said, eyeing an emerald green minidress in the window. "What a gorgeous color."

Jake stopped. "Yeah," he said, "green's a nice color, all right."

"Would you mind if I went inside for a little while?" she asked, looking up at him hopefully. "This is my favorite store."

"No problem." Jake stuck his hands in his pockets. "Take your time. I'll wait out here."

Kate went inside and found the same dress on one of the racks. Made from a soft silk chiffon, the dress had an empire waist and a skirt that flared out in many layers. It would look fabulous on her slim frame, Kate knew, but she didn't really need a formal dress.

"Would you like to try it on, miss?" a saleswoman asked.

"I'd love to," Kate said, "but someone's waiting for me outside." From where she stood, she could see Jake patiently waiting, watching the shoppers go by. She studied his strong profile for a moment. He was handsome in a calm, stable way, she thought, and patient, too. She returned the dress to the rack and went outside to join him. "Okay," she said to Jake, approaching him from behind. "Thanks for waiting."

"No prob." He offered her his arm again.

She took his arm and they headed toward the pizza place at the food court.

"Let me guess. You look like a guy who eats pepperoni and extra cheese. Am I right?" she asked.

"Hey, yeah." Jake took a step back and looked at her. "How'd you know?"

Kate shrugged, laughing. She and Jake were right for each other. She'd never been so sure of anything in her entire life. "Maybe we knew each other in another lifetime."

They ordered one large pepperoni and cheese pizza and two Cokes, and found a table at the far end of the food court.

"You like it spicy, right?" Kate said, holding up a large plastic bottle of crushed red pepper.

"Right again," he said, nodding. "Go for it."

Kate shook red pepper over the whole pizza. "So, what are you doing this weekend?" she asked.

Jake shrugged. "I haven't really thought about it yet. What about you?"

"Well, I'm working on a new project," she said. "A collage of some of my old black-and-white photos." She paused. "But other than that, I don't really have anything planned."

"Well, maybe we can do something over the weekend, then. Like, maybe you could show me your collage or something."

"I'm flattered that you're interested," Kate said, "but you might have to wait till next week for that. I don't think it'll be finished yet."

"Of course I'm interested," Jake said. "I've never known a photographer before."

Kate chewed on her slice of pizza contentedly. This guy was almost too good to be true.

"So how did you get into photography?" he asked.

"Well, actually," Kate began, "my ex-boyfriend turned me on to it, like, two years ago."

Jake took a sip of Coke. "Really?"

Kate nodded. She hadn't thought about the past in a while, and no one on the island had seemed too interested. Until now, she'd kind of enjoyed forgetting. But she wanted to be up-front with Jake. "He was a real photo buff. Camera club . . . you know."

"How long did you go out with him?"

Kate glanced at her pizza. "My whole junior year."

"You really liked this guy, huh?" Jake said softly.

"Yeah, I really did. Actually, I was totally in love with him. But it got kind of crazy in the end."

Jake looked at her with a serious expression.

"His ex-girlfriend decided that she wanted him back."

"So he left you?" Jake asked cautiously.

"I left *him*," Kate said ruefully, "after she hassled me for weeks."

"She *hassled* you?" Jake said in disbelief.

"She followed us, called me constantly, threatened me . . . it was horrible."

"God, that's incredible," Jake said. "I can't believe anyone would do that."

"It was a total nightmare," Kate said. "I felt so . . . so unsafe and insecure all the time. Like I had to keep looking over my shoulder."

Jake put down his slice of pizza. "I bet."

"You know, that's one of the things I like about you," Kate said pensively. "I always feel so safe with you. I guess it's because you helped me that night."

Jake cleared his throat and leaned forward. For a moment Kate thought he was going to kiss her, but instead he gently laid a hand on hers. "Kate," he said in a low voice, "I'm really glad I make you feel safe . . . but I can't help wondering . . ."

Kate looked into his eyes.

"Well," Jake said, shifting in his seat, "sometimes I think what you have for me is just some kind of weird fixation."

"Fixation? What do you mean?"

"I mean, if Lucas had carried you out that night, you'd be after him," Jake explained. "And if it had been Benjamin, you would have fixated on Benjamin, right?"

Kate nodded thoughtfully, then sighed. "You're right," she admitted. "At least you're partly right. In fact," she said, her face hot with embarrassment, "at first

I thought it *was* Benjamin who'd come to help me."

"So you went after him?"

Kate blushed as she spoke. "You could say that. I sort of kissed him, too."

"Like, a kiss?" Jake exclaimed. "A real kiss?"

Kate nodded and put her face in her hands. "God! I was so embarrassed."

"See?" Jake said in an accusing tone. "That's what I mean. I don't think you really like *me*, Jake McRoyan. I think you're really in love with . . . with . . . I don't know." He threw his hands up in frustration.

"No, Jake," Kate said, looking into his brown eyes. "I mean, I liked you even before I found out that it was you who'd helped me that night."

Jake looked at her doubtfully. "Then why did you turn me down when I asked you out that night at Louise's party?"

"Because at the time I thought it was Benjamin who had come to my rescue," Kate tried to explain. "But I wanted to say yes. Really I did."

"Jakie!" Kate suddenly heard a shrill voice coming up behind her back. "I was just thinking about you, and then I saw you sitting here." Lara took her large purse off her shoulder and put it on the table. "Isn't that strange?" she said, widening her eyes.

Kate didn't know Lara very well, but she knew that she and Jake had dated. "Hi, Lara," she said.

"Oh, hi," Lara said dismissively. "Mind if I join you for a minute?" she asked Jake. She positioned herself on the edge of Jake's bench, forcing him to slide over.

"Actually . . ." Jake shifted his gaze to Kate. "We were just getting ready to leave."

"Ohhh," Lara said, whining with exaggerated disappointment. "It'll just take a minute. It's been so long since we've chatted."

Jake nodded resignedly and gave Kate an apologetic look. "So what's up, Lara?"

"Well," she said, beaming, "I just heard about the prom—Zoey mentioned she was going—and I was wondering if you wanted to go with me."

Kate looked at Jake. She couldn't believe Lara had just come right out and asked him. And it suddenly occurred to Kate that *she* wouldn't mind going to the prom with Jake. She could buy that new dress and they could have a fancy dinner beforehand.

For a second Jake's eyes darted back and forth between Kate and Lara. "I'm not going to the prom," he said smoothly. "I've got other plans."

"Really?" Lara's eyes widened. "But it's such a big deal. You have to go."

Jake shook his head. "No, Lara, I don't," he said with finality.

Kate frowned. So much for going to the prom. She thought about the emerald green dress in the window and pictured Jake in his tuxedo. It would have been so perfect. . . .

Christopher remade Lucas's bed and circled his bedroom, stacking papers and magazines in neat piles, folding various clothing items, and dusting furniture. Mrs. Cabral had let him in and he had been waiting for Lucas to get home for the last half hour. Christopher knew it was a little strange that he was picking up after his friend, but he had become accustomed to the austere surroundings at boot camp, and he couldn't stand the sight of clutter. And anyway, he felt too edgy to just sit still.

A moment later Lucas arrived. His eyes widened in surprise when he saw Christopher. "Picked up some guerilla tactics in the army? How did you get in here, man?" He glanced down at the floor. "So that's what my carpet looks like," he said.

Christopher laughed. "I've just been here a few minutes. Your mom let me in. I needed to talk to you and I thought I'd just put things in order while I was here."

"Well, thanks," Lucas said, still scanning the room.

"So . . ." Christopher sat down on a chair. "What's Zoey up to?"

Lucas took off his shoes and sprawled across his bed. "She had to go help out at the restaurant. I'll probably go see her later."

Christopher stood up and dragged the chair over to Lucas's desk. "You're going to the prom this weekend, aren't you?" he asked.

"Yeah," Lucas said. He pulled off a sock and threw it on the floor. "Why? Are you and Eesh going, too?"

"Uh, yeah," Christopher said. "Aisha just told me about it last night."

Lucas tossed his other sock on the floor. "Great," he said. "Then I won't be the sole representative of Chatham Island manhood. The responsibility was beginning to weigh on me."

"I'm kind of looking forward to it, actually," Christopher said. "Where I come from, it wasn't exactly cool to be going to the prom."

Lucas made an indistinct sound in his throat. "Well, I hate to break it to you, but it's not the coolest thing around here, either."

Christopher raised his eyebrows. "Oh, it's not? Not even for the illustrious homecoming king?"

Lucas shook his head. "Please don't remind me. I've erased that humiliating experience from my memory. I remember every single traumatic moment at Youth Authority, but homecoming night is just a blur."

Aisha had nominated Lucas for the position of

64

homecoming king and to his chagrin, he had actually won. Though he had blown off the homecoming game, he had been forced to attend the dance afterward for the crowning ceremony. Dancing with Louise Kronenberger, the homecoming queen, while the entire student body hooted and gawked was something Lucas had tried to forget.

Christopher chuckled. "So, I guess I'm going to have to get a tux or something, huh?"

"Yeah," Lucas said. "There's this place not far from the ferry terminal in Weymouth . . . I can give you their address."

"Thanks," Christopher said. He shuffled nervously through the papers on Lucas's desk. "Listen, I want to ask you something. Do you know anything about this guy Aisha's been seeing?" He tried to keep his voice as casual as he could.

"Uh . . ." Lucas hesitated.

Christopher hated putting his friend on the spot, but he had to know. "Come on, buddy," he urged. "I swear I won't tell Aisha you said anything."

Lucas looked uncomfortable. "I, ah . . . I don't really know anything about that."

"But you know she's been seeing someone, right?"

Lucas nodded. "Zoey mentioned some guy once," he said, "but she didn't really fill me in on the details, and I didn't ask."

Christopher leaned against the edge of Lucas's desk, his arms crossed in front of him. "But do you know if she's been seeing him long?"

"Christopher, man, I swear," Lucas said. "I really don't know."

"Well, what *do* you know about him?" Christopher demanded, pushing himself up to sit on the desk.

"Nothing, really," Lucas said. "I just know that Eesh

went to the movies with him or something . . . I don't even know his name."

Christopher scratched his chin. "I guess it's a good sign that you've never met him," he said thoughtfully.

"Well, actually," Lucas said slowly, "I think I *did* meet him at Louise Kronenberger's house, but I can't be sure it was the same guy. All I know is . . ." His voice trailed off—as though, Christopher thought, he was hiding something.

"What?" Christopher said, hopping off the desk. "What?"

Lucas hesitated. "Oh. Never mind. Forget about it," he said, avoiding Christopher's eyes. "It's stupid."

"No," Christopher insisted. "Just tell me what you know."

Lucas blew some air out of his mouth. "Okay," he said, "but don't get upset."

"I can handle it," Christopher said grimly.

"Well," Lucas began, "we were playing spin-the-bottle, believe it or not, and . . . and . . ."

"And what?"

"And Eesh ended up kissing some guy." Lucas gave Christopher a worried look.

"That's *it?*" Christopher said, relieved. "That doesn't sound so bad. I mean, that's what happens when you play spin-the-bottle, right? I mean, if my memory serves me correctly. It's been a while since I've played." He looked at Lucas curiously.

"Stop looking at me like that, man," Lucas said with a chuckle. "It was one of those spur-of-the-moment things. You had to be there, okay? But . . ."

"But what?"

"Just so you're not walking into this situation totally blind, you might as well know. Eesh kissed him for a really long time," Lucas mumbled, "like she knew him or something."

"Oh, jeez," Christopher said, throwing his head back and covering his face with his hands. "That really bites."

Christopher

RIGHT NOW IS DEFINITELY THE WRONG
TIME TO BE ASKING ME THAT QUESTION. I
DON'T EVEN KNOW WHAT I'LL BE DOING NEXT
WEEK, MUCH LESS TEN YEARS FROM NOW.

IT'S HARD TO BELIEVE THAT ONLY A
WEEK AGO I WAS ON A VERY CLEAR AND CER-
TAIN PATH. THE U.S. ARMY PATH. IT
DOESN'T GET MUCH STRAIGHTER OR NAR-
ROWER THAN THAT.

SO NOW THAT I'VE LEFT THAT PATH FOR
ONE THAT'S LIKELY TO TURN OUT TO BE
CIRCUITOUS AND MEANDERING, I FEEL LIKE
I'M FLOUNDERING. (OF COURSE, I'M NOT
ABOUT TO ADMIT THAT TO ANYONE.)

EVERYTHING IN MY LIFE IS UNCERTAIN.
HELL, I DON'T EVEN FEEL SURE ABOUT THIS
WHOLE THING WITH AISHA.

BUT, ACTUALLY, NOT KNOWING HOW IT'S
ALL GOING TO TURN OUT IS NOT BAD. IN
FACT, PART OF THE REASON I LEFT THE
ARMY IS THAT I GOT SICK OF THE PRE-
DICTABILITY OF IT ALL AND THE ABSOLUTE
CERTAINTY ABOUT WHAT WAS GOING TO HAP-
PEN NEXT. TO PUT IT PLAINLY, IT GOT TO
BE BORING.

SO WHERE DO I SEE MYSELF TEN YEARS
FROM NOW? ALL I CAN SAY FOR SURE IS

THAT I WILL BE A CIVILIAN (I.E., NOT IN UNIFORM), AND THAT I WILL HAVE MADE IT THROUGH COLLEGE AND GRADUATE SCHOOL, AND THAT AISHA WILL BE MY WIFE, AND THAT I WILL BE THE OWNER OF MY OWN BUSINESS, AND THAT THE BUSINESS WILL BE VERY SUCCESSFUL.

QUITE A STATEMENT FOR SOMEONE WHO DOESN'T EVEN HAVE A JOB, ISN'T IT?

Nine

Nina felt her heart accelerate as the sun slipped lower and lower toward the horizon, and the realization that she was totally and utterly lost finally hit her. Portland certainly wasn't the big, bustling city she remembered, with people everywhere—or maybe she had just wandered too far from the center.

It had been nearly half an hour since a woman on the street had given her directions for a "shortcut" to the waterfront area, and Nina hadn't passed another person since then. A few cars had passed her, but no taxis, and now Nina cursed herself for not taking a map along with her. And she cursed the imbecilic woman whose fault this all was.

Maple Street, the sign on top of a post said. *Well,* she thought, *at least I know I'm on Maple Street.* It *sounded* safe. But she was looking for Spring Street, where the woman said she would find several "delicious" seafood restaurants and a few "really quaint" antique shops. Nina had already tried backtracking, but that had only led her to an even more desolate and dangerous-looking area with boarded-up buildings and garbage in the streets. Maple Street at least looked sort of lived in, though it was clearly more a commercial area than a residential one.

"Okay, Nina," she said to herself. "Don't panic." She

took a deep breath and picked up her pace. "So what if it's dark—okay, pitch black—and you're totally lost in a strange city?" *It's not like you have anyone to go home to.* "Everything's going to be fine." *Hey, maybe Benjamin will be really sorry if I'm found dismembered and dead in a ditch. That'll be* some *consolation. Hmmm . . . would he even go to my funeral?*

She took several more deep breaths, dismissing her morbid thoughts, and decided that prayer wasn't such a bad thing. Too bad she didn't know any prayers. She could really use the help.

Walking as fast as she could in her well-worn combat boots, she turned a corner, smashed right into someone, and fell backward, hitting a fire hydrant before landing on the pavement.

"Ow!" she yelled, scrambling to get up and run.

A man was standing above her, waving a long object menacingly over her head. What was it—a bat, or was it a lead pipe?

Nina quickly got up, shielding her face with her arms. "Don't hurt me," she begged, terrified. "Please don't hurt me." She was shaking and very close to tears.

The man leaned over to get a closer look at her, then he dropped his weapon, a slender cane, and laughed derisively.

Nina cautiously lowered her arms and for a moment just stared at the weather-beaten old man wearing a holey Panama hat and about four layers of shirts. At six feet, and with a heavy salt-and-pepper beard, he was grizzled and intimidating. "I'm sorry," she said meekly. "I didn't see you."

"Next time watch where you're goin'," he said grumpily, stooping to pick up his cane.

Nina nodded and glanced over her shoulder to see if there was anywhere she could run to. Her breath was shallow and irregular, and she seemed to have lost the feeling in all her extremities.

"Say," he said, his face just inches from hers, "what're you doin' here, anyway?"

Nina swallowed hard and wondered if it was a good idea to tell him she was lost. "I'm . . . I'm trying to find Spring Street," she squeaked.

"You can't get there from here," he said gruffly, pointing at their surroundings with his cane.

Nina sighed in despair. "Can you tell me where this road goes?" she asked hopefully.

"Don't go nowhere," he responded. "Stays right where she is."

The man was loony, but Nina didn't really have many options. Maybe she just needed to rephrase the question. "Well, is the waterfront area far?"

"Waal," he said, scratching his beard and squinting, "I'd say about twenty-five thousand miles."

He definitely had one or two screws loose. "Twenty-five thousand miles?" she repeated.

"Sure," he said as if it were obvious, "the way yer facin'."

Nina shook her head. Having grown up on a tiny island where she knew practically every stone, the situation at hand was particularly disconcerting. "I don't understand."

"You from outta state?" he asked, eyeing her suspiciously.

"No," Nina said truthfully. "I just don't know this area too well."

"You oughta relax first," he said. "I ain't gonna hurt you."

That's just what the deranged stalker on All My Children *said to Brooke when he kidnapped her,* she thought. *And he was planning to dress Brooke in his*

72

grandmother's wedding gown and force her to listen to Sting sing "Every Breath You Take" over and over again until she cracked. Nina made herself exhale when she realized she'd been holding her breath. "I am relaxed," she said, feeling incredibly tense.

The man's beard shifted slightly, and it sort of looked like he might be smiling. "Turn 'round," he said.

Oh, my God, it's happening, Nina thought. *Isn't that a Bonnie Tyler song?* "Wh-what do you mean?" Nina said, panicking.

"I told you," he said impatiently. "Yer facin' the wrong way."

Oh. Nina turned around slowly, her body rigid.

"Good," the man said. "Now, you see that stop sign over there?"

"Yes," Nina said, reminding herself to breathe.

"See it?" the man said, sidling up next to her and pointing.

Nina nodded vigorously. "Yes."

"Waal, if you go over there and turn left . . . no, wait. I mean right. Turn right."

Nina didn't dare turn her head to look at him. The guy was crazy, and she was afraid any sudden movement would set him off.

"You listenin'?" he said, looking her up and down.

"Yes," she answered as calmly as she could. "Turn right at the stop sign."

"If you do that," he said, "you'll be on Spring Street."

"Thank you," Nina managed, shifting her gaze to the man without moving her head.

"Yer welcome," the man said. "And by the way, I'm Bill."

"Well, thanks," she said again.

"What's yer name?"

"Nina," she said nervously. "Nina Temple."

"You Shirley's daughter?" he asked, his blue eyes lighting up.

"No, no, I'm not," she said. "Thanks again." She took a step backward. "I have to get going. It's late."

"You take care now, Miss Temple," he said, waving his cane around. "And next time watch where yer goin'."

Nina ran to the stop sign and turned right. Just one block away, on top of a post, was a sign: Spring Street. Shaking uncontrollably now, Nina sat down on the curb. In all her life, she had never felt so terrified as she had just minutes before. Tears sprang to her eyes as she realized how utterly vulnerable she was outside of Chatham Island, where it was always quiet, safe, and reassuringly familiar.

What am I doing here? she asked herself. *This is crazy!* For a fleeting moment Nina felt an overwhelming desire to go back home—but she quickly dismissed that option. Over the last forty-eight hours she had gradually arrived at a decision: She would never look back. She would find herself a job somewhere, and she would make it on her own. For as long as Benjamin was still on Chatham Island, Nina had no choice but to build a life of her own somewhere else. As difficult as it would be, it was better than spending the rest of her life longing for what she and Benjamin would never have again.

Zoey sat at her desk in her dormered window, rereading the story she'd started to write the night before. Not bad, she thought. Jane Austen would approve. And the process of writing it had been sort of cathartic, not that she didn't still feel miserable about Nina's departure.

Zoey poised her pen over her notebook, concentrated hard to put herself in an early-nineteenth-century frame of mind, and picked up from where she'd left off. . . .

"You need not think about this unfortunate situation any longer, my dear," said Chloe to a weeping Tina. "It is folly to continue in this vein, weeping and carrying on as though it should mean the very death of you."

Until, finally, Tina could no longer bear the torment. The realization that she had been abandoned, first by her true love, and now by her most intimate friend, hit her with dreadful force, and she decided that she must flee the island, and forsake her once happy and secure home for the farthest reaches of the earth.

Chloe was horror-struck and could scarcely comprehend this awful news. "Oh, poor creature! Poor Tina!" she cried. "How unfeeling I have been! How selfish!"

Chloe knew that her conduct had not been that of a true friend. In pressing Tina to overcome the hurdles of her broken heart, she had acted wrongly and had done Tina nothing but disservice. It was a most unpardonable offense!

Tina had always been a loyal and constant friend to Chloe. At times of cheerlessness, Tina had never failed to provide felicity and mirth. She had made her laugh; she had sung her delightful tunes while playing the pianoforte; and she had accompanied her on countless carriage rides and long walks. And, *unlike the deplorable Chloe, Tina never tired of listening to her friend's worries, always encouraging Chloe to unburden herself at her expense.*

It was rather too late to retract her ill-mannered behavior toward poor Tina, so instead Chloe committed herself to the resolution that

Zoey dropped her pen. That what? What was she going to do for Nina? What could she possibly do to redeem herself?

There was a knock on the door. "Are you there, Zo?" *Lucas.* "Yeah," Zoey called out. "Come on in."

"What are you up to?" He closed the door behind him and crossed the room to give her a kiss.

Zoey turned her notebook facedown. "Just writing."

"Really? What are you writing?" He peered curiously at the notebook, and even though the writing was covered up, Zoey instinctively pressed it tightly against the desktop.

"Oh, just a stupid story," she said dismissively.

He made a grab for the notebook, but Zoey snatched it away before he could get to it. "About what?" he said. "Come on. Let me see."

"Lucas!" Zoey snapped. "We just had a discussion about this . . . *problem* two days ago. Lay off."

"It's not your diary, Zo," he said, looking hurt. "I'm just curious about what you're writing."

She gave him a threatening look.

"Jeez," he said, backing off and flopping on her bed. "Fine."

Zoey was surprised—and maybe a little flattered, too—by how disappointed Lucas seemed. She was amazed that he was even interested. "Okay," she said gently. "But it's silly—so you can't laugh."

Lucas propped himself up with a pillow. "You'll let me see it?" he said eagerly.

"Maybe when it's done," she said, embarrassed. "Right now I won't let anyone see it. It still needs work."

A shadow of disappointment crossed Lucas's face. "Oh. I thought you were going to show it to me."

"Well, I can tell you about it. It's about Nina," Zoey said plainly. "But I sort of fictionalized it a bit, and I tried to write it in Jane Austen's style." She paused, wrinkling her nose at him. "Pretty stupid, huh?"

"So why won't you show it to me?"

"I don't know," Zoey admitted. "Because you'll think it's totally dumb, I guess."

Lucas looked at her blankly. "But isn't Jane Austen the one you keep going on and on about? The one whose books they keep making movies out of?"

"You got it," Zoey said.

"So why would I think it's stupid?" he asked, sounding genuinely confused. "I bet it's really good."

"Just *because*," Zoey said, exasperated.

Lucas shook his head in bewilderment. "You are so strange, Zo."

Zoey sighed loudly. "Okay, okay," she said. "I'll show it to you, but you have to wait till I'm finished with it."

Lucas shrugged. "Fine. I'll wait."

"In the meantime," Zoey said, coming over to the

bed and lying on her stomach next to him, "I need a back rub." She took his hands and put them on her shoulders. "Especially there."

Lucas straddled her and began pressing his knuckles into the knots in her shoulders.

"Mmm," she said, feeling as if her muscles were melting off her bones. "That feels great."

"So what are you writing about Nina?"

"Lucas," Zoey said, craning her neck around, "why are you so interested?"

"I don't know," he said as he kneaded. "Maybe because I'm interested in *you*."

Zoey lifted her upper body and twisted so she could look at him. "Just about why she ran away and stuff."

"Oh," he said, "you mean the stuff about Benjamin."

"Yeah," she said, twisting back around. "And me. You know, like if I had been a better friend to her, maybe she wouldn't have run away and all."

"Zo." Lucas leaned forward awkwardly to make eye contact with her. "It's not your fault."

"Lucas, there's nothing you can say to make me feel better," she said. "I just wish I knew how to make it up to her."

Lucas sighed. "So you'll be a better listener from now on."

"Yeah." Zoey smiled forlornly. "I'll be a better listener."

It was rather too late to retract her ill-mannered behavior toward poor Nina, so instead Chloe committed herself to the resolution

that she would repress
her selfishness and be
good to Tina for all the
rest of her life, and
endeavor to dedicate herself
to promoting Tina's happiness and comfort; that is,
should Tina ever return to
Chamden.

When several days
passed, and Tina still had
not returned, Chloe's
wretchedness increased. Her
only source of consolation
was her resolution to here-
after behave in a more con-
siderate and thoughtful
manner, and in the hope
that however trying this
lesson was, it would leave
her wiser and with a
deeper understanding of
herself.

Ten

Aisha waved good-bye to Zoey, Lucas, Claire, and Benjamin at the ferry landing and headed for the town beach. The day before, Christopher had promised to prepare an after-school picnic, and she had agreed to go straight to the beach from the ferry.

It was the day Aisha was supposed to break up with David, and she really had intended to, but somehow she just hadn't been able to bring herself to do it. And even though Christopher hadn't said anything more about David when she'd seen him the night before—in fact, he'd been strangely silent on the topic—she worried that he would be really angry when she told him that she still hadn't done what she had promised.

As soon as she climbed over a sand dune, she saw him busily spreading out a picnic blanket over the sand and pinning down the corners with rocks. The thought occurred to her that she almost never saw him in an attitude of repose. In fact, the only time she'd ever seen him rest had been when he was recovering from being beaten up by those skinheads. She had shown him then that she would be there for him, that he could count on her.

Please don't be mad. I'll do it tomorrow, she silently

promised. A cool breeze stirred up the dune grass around her ankles as she walked toward him.

"Hi," she said when she got to the edge of the blanket. "What a gorgeous day." She took a deep breath, filling her lungs with the ocean air.

Christopher turned around and immediately wrapped his strong arms around her. "Hungry?" he asked, giving her a quick kiss on the lips.

Aisha dumped her backpack on the blanket and knelt down, surveying the goodies Christopher had carefully laid out. "I am now." He had laid out potato salad, sandwiches, fruit, and chilled bottles of Snapple iced tea. "Everything looks *so* good."

Christopher sat on the blanket next to her, twisted open a bottle of peach iced tea, and handed it to her. "Only the best for you," he said, smiling.

"Thanks." Aisha laughed and took the bottle. She hoped he'd forgotten about her promise.

Christopher stretched out across the blanket, propping himself up on one elbow. "So, did you get your bio lab done?"

"Yup," Aisha said. "I stayed up half the night to finish it, but it's in now. What about you?" she said, trying to shift the focus of the conversation to Christopher. "How was the job search today?"

"Very good, actually. I found a job."

"That's great!" Aisha exclaimed. She examined the serious expression in his eyes and felt a surge of guilt. "Why aren't you excited?" she asked cautiously.

"Oh, I'm very happy about the job," he assured her. "I'm going to be waiting tables at this new restaurant that's opening where Angelino's used to be, on Exchange Street."

"Yeah?" Aisha said, motioning for him to continue.

"But there is a bad side," he said. "Their grand opening is on Saturday night. *This* Saturday night."

"Oh," Aisha said. "The prom."

"I can still go," Christopher hurried on. "But I'm going to have to be late. I can probably meet you there by ten."

Aisha stuck her lower lip out in a pout, but part of her felt strangely relieved. She really was disappointed that Christopher would have to miss half of the biggest event of the year, but now she wondered if it was absolutely necessary to *not* go with David. She'd put off breaking the bad news to David for so long, it would be cruel to do it now, when it was too late for him to find another date. How could she leave him dateless for the only prom he would ever have in his life? But it looked as if there was a way around it after all. *Too good to be true,* Aisha thought.

Aloud she said, "Can't you be there sooner?"

Christopher looked at her apologetically. "I'm really, really sorry, Eesh," he said, "but I need this job, and if I'm not there for the opening, they'll give it to someone else."

Aisha sighed loudly. "I understand."

Christopher took her hand. "I'll make it up to you, okay?"

Aisha nodded and tried not to smile too widely. This wasn't working out so badly. The urgency of breaking up with David had suddenly been lifted *and* Christopher seemed to have forgotten that it was Wednesday, the day she had promised to do *it*.

"Now that that's over with," Christopher said, "don't you have some news you want to share with me?"

Aisha felt her heart skip a beat. "No," she said in a questioning tone. "What do you mean?"

"Today's Wednesday."

This wasn't going to be so easy after all. "Oh, is it?" she said, laughing nervously. "God, it's amazing." She shook her head. "Sometimes I don't even know what day it is."

"Come on, Eesh," he said. "Stop fooling around. Did you do it?"

"Um . . . yeah," she said, looking away. "I've stopped seeing him. I mean, I *see* him at school and all, but I'm not *seeing* him anymore." There. It was out, and she'd sort of lied—but not really, because she *had* stopped seeing him. In fact, she'd been avoiding him all week.

Christopher looked at her doubtfully. "Are you sure?"

"Yes," she said staunchly.

"Then why aren't you looking me in the eye?"

Aisha forced herself to look straight into his dark, serious eyes. "I stopped seeing him," she said, trying very hard to enunciate the words clearly and hold his gaze.

"Okay," Christopher said. "I believe you."

Aisha tried her best to seem lighthearted. But deep down she felt horrible. Not only had she just deceived Christopher; unsuspecting David was going to be coming to Chatham Island on the next ferry to tutor Kalif, Aisha's fourteen-year-old brother, and he was expecting to see her. And when he realized she wasn't home, he was going to be really hurt.

But at least she wasn't going to have to break up with him yet, and at least she wasn't going to have to abandon him totally on prom night. The problem was, how was she going to make David leave halfway through the prom?

Aisha

I really hate these kinds of questions. The Princeton rep asked me this one when I interviewed with her in Weymouth. I gave a straightforward answer, that in ten years I would be either in med school or working on my Ph.D., but I don't really know. I mean, when someone asks this kind of question, there's no way you can give a real answer, because there's no way you can predict the future.

Maybe I'm just too much of a math and science geek, and maybe I'm just so deficient imagination-wise that I can't even hazard a guess, but I can't help it. These kinds of questions really frustrate me. Which is probably part of the reason I'm handling this Christopher/David thing so poorly. Having two dates to the prom is kind of like having two solutions to a problem where both solutions are completely correct. I can't choose one solution over the other because they're both valid, so why should I?

Eleven

Nina adjusted her backpack over her shoulder as she waited in line to board the Greyhound bus headed for Portsmouth, New Hampshire. She'd tried to catch the express earlier in the day but missed it because she'd gotten lost—again. Now she was going to have to stop in a million dinky towns along the way, which annoyed her even though she wasn't in any rush to go anywhere.

It had been three days since she left Chatham Island, but Nina felt as if she'd been gone for weeks. And although the memory of Benjamin and Kate kissing still haunted her, she did feel more distant from it now, and more in control of her emotions. Being away from it all, away from home, was her only chance for survival. She desperately wanted to forget, and it was the only way she knew how to stop the memories.

But somewhere in the back of her mind, Nina also knew that running away wasn't always the best solution to a problem. Right after her mother had died, her father had sent her to live with her uncle and aunt, and her uncle had molested her. For years Nina had managed to repress her anger and feelings of guilt, but it wasn't until she finally stood up for herself and confronted him that she'd begun to heal from the horrific experience.

Still, facing Benjamin and Kate was too much for Nina even to imagine. She was certain that she'd fall apart, and the last thing she wanted was for them to pity her. No, Nina would never put herself in that position. She would never give them the satisfaction. Not now. Not ever.

She sighed, feeling fatigue suddenly wash over her. She'd forgotten to eat before coming to the bus station, and she badly needed some sleep. *Well, at least I've lost some weight,* she said to herself wryly. *The Benjamin Passmore diet plan: guaranteed to make you miserable and lose ten pounds overnight, or your money back.*

Finally it was her turn to board the bus, and Nina laboriously climbed the steps.

"Ever wonder why all bus stairs are built for people who are nine feet tall?"

Nina turned around. A woman in her early twenties was carrying a garment bag and smiling at her. "All the time," Nina said crankily. *Great. She's probably planning to tell me about a shortcut to Portsmouth.* She made her way to the back of the bus and took a window seat.

The woman took the aisle seat next to her. "Ahhhh," she said to no one in particular. "It feels so good to sit down."

Is that the beginning of a very long monologue? Nina wondered. "Mmm-hmmm," Nina said aloud, hoping that that sort of nonresponse would discourage the woman from going on.

"So," the woman said, ignoring the fact that Nina had reclined her seat and closed her eyes. "Where are you headed?"

Nina opened her eyes and looked at the woman, who was folding a blue blazer neatly in her lap. "Portsmouth," she said.

"Are you from Portsmouth?" the woman asked.

"No." It was no use. This was obviously one determined woman. "I'm from Maine."

"Really?" the woman said, facing Nina. "Portland?"

"No. Chatham Island." Nina unzipped her windbreaker and slipped its sleeves off her arms.

"Oh!" the woman said, lighting up. "Chatham Island. I know it."

"You do?" Nina asked, surprised.

"Yeah," the woman said. "I have a friend who just moved there a few months ago. I hear it's a beautiful little place . . . hey, maybe you know her."

"There's a chance," Nina conceded. "There are only three hundred year-round residents in the whole town."

"Well, maybe, then," the woman said. "Her name's Lara McAvoy."

"You know Lara?" *This preppy-looking woman with the perky bob knows Lara?*

"Uh-huh," the woman said. "She's a pretty good friend of mine. I used to work with her in a deli."

"Oh," Nina said thoughtfully. "You must be from Kittery."

"Yeah, I am," the woman said, nodding. "So you know Lara well. Isn't she just great?"

Nina instinctively shook her head in denial as she suddenly felt her anonymity slipping away. "I don't know her all that well, actually. I've just heard her name mentioned," she said, the lie making her flush a little.

"But you know she's from Kittery?" the woman said in wonder.

"Well, yeah." Nina struggled to come up with a

plausible explanation. "We were talking about Kittery when her name came up."

The woman appeared to believe her. "Have you ever been to Kittery? You should visit someday," the woman said. "We have a historic naval yard that they still use for shipbuilding. It's kind of neat."

Nina nodded, a polite smile pasted onto her face.

"So what are you going to do in Portsmouth?" the woman asked.

"Well, uh," Nina said, quickly scanning through her memory for Portsmouth trivia, "I just thought I'd, uh—" She coughed. "Excuse me. Um, I just thought I'd look at some of the paintings in Strawbery Banke," she said, mentally patting herself on the back for remembering the name of the famous restoration project in Portsmouth. "I'm an art student," she added, confidently elaborating on her lie.

"Oh, how wonderful!" the woman said effusively. "You should definitely meet Lara, then. She paints the most beautiful portraits."

Nina began to wonder if they were talking about the same Lara McAvoy. "Really?" She pictured a drunk Lara in her tight acid-washed jeans, her dirty-blond hair limp and lank.

"Really. She has so much talent," the woman said.

Nina cleared her throat. "Well," she said, "I guess I'm going to have to look her up when I get back home."

The woman's smile widened as she offered Nina her hand. "I'm Jill, by the way."

"Nina," Nina said, shaking her hand. "Nina Temple."

The world was just too small. Nina couldn't get away from Chatham Island even when she was away from it.

* * *

The ferry's whistle shrilled as it pulled into the Chatham Island ferry slip. Jake positioned himself right next to the exit so that he would be the first one off. It had taken him all day to decide, but he had finally resolved to ask Kate to the prom, and he wanted to get it over with quickly, before he lost his nerve.

Jake watched impatiently as the deckhands began to lower the gangway. The process seemed to take much longer than usual, and Jake could hardly resist the urge to go help them. He nervously tapped a sneakered foot against the wooden deck and tried to send them telepathic messages to get on with it. *Faster. Faster.*

When they finally had the gangway in place, Jake ran across it, his bulky form rattling the narrow metal platform beneath him. From the ferry landing, he headed straight down Exchange Street toward Lucas's house, where Kate was staying. He hoped she was home, but more than that, he hoped she wouldn't turn him down. All day he had been stressed about the decision to ask her or not ask her—throughout his classes and especially through the AA meeting right after school.

Although Kate seemed to really like him, she was also a little unpredictable and, well, strange. Even after having pizza with her, Jake wasn't at all convinced that she was interested in *him* and not her fantasy guy. His doubt stemmed from the fact that she hadn't been interested until she found out he was the one who had taken care of her the night she was knocked unconscious—although Kate claimed she had been interested. And he couldn't help but feel that if it had been Lucas who'd saved her, *Lucas* would have been the object of her affections, or Benjamin, or whoever.

Jake sucked in his breath before ringing the Cabrals' doorbell. He practiced what he was going to say while waiting for the door to open: *Kate, will you go to the prom with me? Kate, would you like to go to the prom with me this weekend? Will you be my date to the prom? May I have the honor of escorting you to—*

Jake jerked his head back in surprise when the door suddenly opened and Kate was right in front of him.

"Jake!" she said happily. "What a nice surprise."

"Uh, hi, Kate," he said, irrationally worried that she might have overheard his thoughts a moment before. "Can I, uh, come in for a sec?"

She stepped back with a huge grin. "Please," she said. "And I hope it's for more than a second."

Jake chuckled nervously as he stepped inside and followed her to the living room. He sat down on the sofa and studied the worn upholstery, suddenly feeling incredibly scared. *Ask her now and get it over with,* he told himself. *Just get straight to the point.*

"Kate," he began, "I was wondering if—" He looked up and was immediately filled with horror. She wasn't even in the room. Where had she gone?

"What did you say, Jake?" she called out from the adjacent kitchen. "I can't hear you."

Jake closed his eyes and slowly shook his head. *God, this is so horrible. I should just forget about it. She's going to say no anyway. I mean, she's older. She probably wouldn't be into some dumb high-school thing, anyway.*

Kate came back into the living room with two glasses of Coke. "I knew you'd want one," she said, handing him a glass. "So I didn't even bother asking. Was I right?"

"Sure," Jake said distractedly. "Um, Kate?"

"Yes?" She sat down next to him on the sofa, her thigh pressing against his.

"Um, I was wondering if you'd like to go to the prom with me this Saturday," Jake said in a rush.

"The prom?" she said. "I thought you said—"

"I just said that to get Lara off my back," he explained.

"Oh, wow," she said, "that's great. I mean, I'd love to go to the prom with you."

A huge grin spread across Jake's face. He leaned back against the sofa, relieved and thrilled. "Great," he said, his nervousness and embarrassment forgotten. "And can I take you to dinner, too?" he asked more confidently.

"Of course," she said excitedly. "Yes."

"But you're going to have to meet me at the ferry in Weymouth. Is that okay with you?"

"No problem," she said. "But why?"

"I have a meeting at school," he said, wondering if it was a good time to tell her that he used to have a problem with alcohol. Finally he decided that it was better to be honest.

"Listen . . . ," he began, then hesitated. "You might have heard about this from Lucas or Zoey or someone, but I have something else to tell you."

Kate looked at him curiously, probably reacting to his suddenly serious tone.

"Kate," he said, trying to find the right approach, "the meeting I'm going to is for AA. Do you know what that is?"

"Alcoholics Anonymous?"

Jake nodded. "I used to have a pretty bad drinking problem," he said, "but I've been sober now for over four months."

Kate looked at him with concern. "I see."

"These meetings help me stay off the alcohol," he continued, "so it's really important that I go to them."

Kate gently took his hand and nodded in understanding.

"Anyway," he finished, "I just thought you should know that."

"Thanks for telling me," she said, moving closer to him and touching his cheek with the back of her hand.

Jake resisted the urge to close his eyes. Her touch felt so good against his skin. But when her hand traveled up into his hair, he succumbed to the feeling, closing his eyes to heighten the incredible sensation.

He felt her kiss him, first tentatively on the cheek, then on the lips. Small, gentle, sweet kisses.

He could smell her scent, too, and Jake felt as if all his senses had been awakened.

He opened his eyes and slipped his arms around her waist, drawing her closer to him. As he did, her eyes closed and her lips parted. Jake pressed his lips against her open mouth and kissed her—a long, deep kiss.

JAKE

I don't usually look that far into the future, but if I had to say, I guess I see myself in ten years in a sports-related field. Maybe married, maybe with a kid.

Sometimes I worry that I'll get an injury that will suddenly end my football career. It happens all the time, and that really scares me. If that happened to me, I'm not sure what I would do. Sports have been my life ever since I can remember. And let's face it, I'm not that good at much else.

Another thing I worry

about is the drinking. It's really been a struggle for me to stay away from alcohol, and though I hope in ten years it won't be such a problem anymore, I know that's unrealistic. Alcoholism is a lifelong disease, and it's difficult for me to accept that I will have to fight it for the rest of my life.

So I guess I don't really know yet what I want out of life. I only know what difficulties I might have to face. But I'm sure it'll turn out okay. I'll take it one day at a time, just like they say in AA.

Twelve

Claire heard Sarah coming up the stairs as she was brushing her teeth in the second-floor bathroom she shared with Nina. Even though Sarah and Aaron had rooms at the Gray's B&B, Sarah spent most of her time at the Geigers' house. *Oh, good,* she thought. *The munchkin is finally turning in for the night.* She quickly finished up the rest of her bedtime routine, then silently slipped down the stairs to her father's study, where she knew she would find him reading.

The door was open, and her father was sitting in his favorite chair, hidden behind a newspaper.

"Hi," Claire said, making an effort to keep her voice down so as not to startle him.

Her father lowered his paper and smiled. He looked tired and drawn, and there were dark circles under his eyes. "Oh, hi, Claire," he said. "It's only nine. Are you going to bed already?"

"Sort of," Claire said. "I have a lot of reading to get through for school tomorrow, so I thought I'd do it in bed."

"Maybe I should go to bed early tonight, too." Her father yawned.

"Good idea," Claire said. "You need the rest. It's been a tough couple of days."

"Yes, it has. That sister of yours has us all crazy with worry."

"No word from Nina today, huh?" Half of her felt bad about introducing the topic. Her father and Sarah had been arguing about Nina for the last two days, and Claire knew that it was placing tremendous stress on her father. But the other half couldn't resist using the sore subject as a means to an end; specifically, a means to end all Geiger-Mendel ties once and for all.

Her father woefully shook his head. "Nothing," he said. "God, I hope she's all right."

Claire went over and sat on the sofa next to him. "Dad," she said in a soothing voice, "I'm sure she's fine."

"I hope you're right." He folded his newspaper and set it aside.

"Well," Claire said, "I think you're doing the right thing by letting her have her space." She paused for a moment. "You're right to think that Nina and *only* Nina can figure this thing out. We could give her all the attention in the world, and she'd still need to pull herself out of this."

Her father remained silent, nodding thoughtfully. "It's just so difficult to know if I'm making the right decision. She's only *sixteen*—and, well, she's so naive."

"She'll call soon," Claire said. "Don't worry."

"Of course I have to worry," he said. "I'm her father. But it does make me feel better that you think I'm doing the right thing."

"You are," Claire said reassuringly. "I'm sure of it."

Her father reached out and squeezed her arm. "Thanks, honey."

"Good night." Claire gave him a kiss on the forehead. "Try to get some rest."

"Good night," he answered wearily.

Claire felt the slightest hint of guilt as she was leaving the room. Her father seemed so worried and depressed about Nina that she began to wonder if it would be too cruel to add more misery to his life by promoting the tension between him and Sarah.

"Oh, and Claire . . . ," her father said just as she reached the door.

Claire turned around to face him. "Yes?"

"Aaron will be coming this weekend to spend Mother's Day with Sarah," he said, smiling as though he was presenting her with good news. "I hope Nina will be back by then."

Any trace of guilt immediately flew out the window as soon as Claire heard Aaron's name, and the hairs on the back of her neck stood up on end. "Oh, great," Claire said, barely disguising her sarcasm. "Good night."

There was no way she was going to end up that egotistical slug's stepsister. No. She was going to come up with a foolproof plan.

Lucas took the stairs, two at a time, up to Zoey's bedroom and knocked on the door. "Zo?" he said. "Zo, are you in there?"

There was no answer, so Lucas opened the door and peered in. The lights were out, which meant Zoey wasn't back from the restaurant yet. He switched on the lights and glanced over at her bed just to be sure she wasn't sleeping. It was unmade, as usual, and Zoeyless, and the Boston Bruins shirt she wore to bed every night was rolled up in a ball where the pillow was supposed to be. The clock radio next to the bed read 9:45, which meant Zoey would be home pretty soon.

Lucas contemplated heading over to the restaurant

and picking her up but decided to stay and take a nap instead. As he was taking off his shoes he noticed that Zoey's diary was conspicuously absent from her desktop. Obviously Zoey didn't have much faith in him and had hidden it away. Her desk, which was built into one of two deep dormers, was cluttered with various papers, pens, and paperbacks, as well as a couple of textbooks.

He grabbed Zoey's pillow, which was near the foot of the bed. Under it was the notebook she'd been writing in the night before, the one she'd refused to show him. Without stopping to think, Lucas reached for it. Only about a quarter of the page facing him was filled with Zoey's perfectly even handwriting. Without reading it, he slipped the notebook under the bed, out of sight, and nestled his head into Zoey's pillow.

Trust, Lucas, a voice in his head kept saying over and over. *If you can't be trusted with the small things, like not snooping into people's things, then how can you be trusted with the bigger stuff?*

He closed his eyes. *But it isn't her diary,* another little voice said. *And she told you she'd show it to you. What's the big deal? She even told you what it's about.*

She'll show it to you when she's ready, the first little voice said. *Be patient.*

It's a story about Nina, for God's sake. What could be so personal about that?

"Yeah," Lucas said aloud as he reached under the bed and grabbed it. *This is different from reading her diary.*

LUCAS

Where do I see myself ten years from now? Well, according to my dad, who thinks I'm a good-for-nothing, I'm never going to amount to much—so sometimes I wonder if I should even try. Or hope.

I must sound like a total loser, and sometimes I think that's what I am. What other name is there for someone who spent two years in Youth Authority for killing Wade McRoyan while driving drunk?

A criminal.

And the fact that I didn't even commit the crime, I was convicted of doesn't really wipe the capital "L" from my forehead.

I've made a lot of mistakes in my life, and yes, I regret making them, because the kind of mistakes I made will still be with me ten years from now, or even twenty-five. Like taking the wrap for Claire in the accident that killed Wade.

But I don't think my dad's right about me. Deep down I know I'm a good person who's learned from his mistakes and will build himself up. And in ten years I won't be under my father's roof anymore, which means I won't have to be constantly reminded that I'm a loser. That'll be a relief.

I wonder will Zoey still love me in ten years?

Thirteen

Holding the cordless phone under her chin, Claire flipped through an old copy of *Mirabella* magazine. She was on her bed, lying on her stomach, and she'd been on hold, waiting for Aaron, for the last ten minutes.

In the background, she could hear the sounds from his boarding-school dormitory: hormonally deranged adolescent boys hooting at Pamela Anderson's breasts while watching *Baywatch*.

She hated calling Aaron in his dorm because more often than not it meant talking to his bone-headed roommate George. This time it sounded as if the whole dorm had piled into their room to watch TV. But Aaron himself had apparently stepped out, and George, rather than going to look for him, had assured Claire that he'd be right back.

Claire sighed in annoyance. She hated waiting for *anybody,* much less Aaron. But it was important that she talk to him before he came in for the weekend. Once again she needed his help in order to pull off the final maneuver that was sure to end Sarah's relationship with Burke Geiger. Claire hated having to ask Aaron, of all people, for favors—but she didn't have a choice. She couldn't do it without him, and besides, Sarah had been such a huge pain in the butt ever since she moved in with the Geigers that Claire couldn't wait to get rid of her. In fact, she suspected that Sarah's moving in had been part of the reason Nina ran away.

That night, before dinner, Claire had picked up a call for her father. It had been a woman named Jordan Kestler, an island resident who owned even more land than her father. Claire didn't know the woman personally, but she had seen her. The woman was in her thirties and looked like a model. Someone who could make Claudia Schiffer feel insecure.

Claire had covered the mouthpiece of the phone and listened quietly. Her father and Jordan were planning to meet at a site near the pond, which Burke was hoping to buy, at ten-thirty on Saturday morning. Claire had immediately realized that this was the opportunity she'd been looking for. All she had to do was get Sarah over there at the appointed time, and Sarah would do the rest herself. With all the Nina-related tension between Sarah and her father, and the doubts that were still plaguing Sarah about Claire's father's alleged infidelity, Claire felt certain that Sarah would go right over the edge when she saw him with Jordan Kestler.

"Hello?" At last Claire finally heard Aaron's voice on the line.

"Well, finally," she said flatly. "It's Claire."

"Claire!" Aaron said. "To what do I owe this honor?"

Claire bristled when she heard the glee in his voice. *Could he possibly be so conceited and obnoxious that he thinks I'm calling just because I want to talk to him?* "I need your help," she said.

"Only if you ask nicely."

Jerk. If Claire hadn't been so desperate to keep him out of her life, she would have hung up on him. "Look, you're coming up to the island this weekend, right?"

"Uh-huh. Friday night till Sunday night."

"Okay," she said. "All I need is for you to take your mother for a spin around the island on Saturday morning."

"Hmmm . . . sounds intriguing," Aaron said. "But I hope this little plan doesn't require me to murder my own mother in some remote wildlife sanctuary or anything like that."

Claire smiled but remained silent. She didn't want him to get the impression that she thought he was funny or anything. Though it seemed impossible for him to be more conceited than he already was, something like that could raise his opinion of himself yet another notch. "I just need you to drive by a piece of land near Big Bite Pond." Big Bite Pond was the body of water that lay right in the middle of the island. It was so vast, it nearly divided Chatham Island in two.

"Why?"

"Because my dad will be there surveying the land with a woman who happens to be quite attractive."

"So you just want me to drive by?" Aaron said. "That's it?"

"That's all it takes," Claire said. "She's the perfect Madeline." Madeline was the pen name Claire had used when she composed the fake love letter she sent to her father.

"And suppose my mother decides to get out of the car and shoot your father with her pearl-handled forty-five," Aaron said. "Where should I dump his body?"

Claire smiled again in spite of herself. Aaron could be pretty funny sometimes, but he was still a slimeball as far as Claire was concerned. "Don't let your mother get out of the car. Just keep on driving."

"So I suppose you're about to tell me exactly when and where," he said.

At first Aaron had been reluctant to participate in

' any of Claire's schemes to break up their parents, but eventually Claire had been able to convince him to cooperate by telling him she would forgive him for cheating on her if he would help her out. But his easy compliance made Claire wonder: Was it possible that Aaron resisted the idea of their families uniting as much as she did? Had Aaron lost all interest in her?

"Eesh," Zoey said the next day in the cafeteria, "you *can't* go to the prom with two dates! It's just not done." She looked at Claire for support, but Claire just shrugged.

"I know it's a little weird, Zo," Aisha conceded, "but don't you think this deserves some consideration? I mean, Christopher's not coming till around ten. I know we can work with this. . . ."

"No, it's not right," Zoey said, shaking her head stubbornly.

"How can I tell David that I can't go to the prom with him?" Aisha argued. "That would be so mean."

"You should have thought about that before you went and asked Christopher to the prom," Zoey said.

"Look, the last thing I want is for you to tell me what I should have done," Aisha said irritably. "Will you just help me figure out what to do?"

"The way I see it, you have only one choice. You have to decide which guy you want to go with, and then you have to tell the other one the truth."

"I can't do that!" Aisha said, stabbing a straw into a cup of soda.

Zoey sighed in exasperation. She and Aisha had been going around in circles on the prom issue since the ferry ride to school that morning. She knew her friend was desperate, but she felt she had to help her see the light.

Claire had her nose buried in *The Great Gatsby* and didn't seem to be listening.

"I know," Aisha said with sudden calm. "I can go to dinner with David and then afterward pretend I'm sick." She looked at Zoey for approval.

"Yeah, right," Zoey scoffed, "and when he decides to go to the prom without you, you'll be there with Christopher."

Aisha frowned. "Oh, you're right . . . but wait!" she said, her face lighting up. "What if I go with David to dinner and the prom, and then have Benjamin or someone call him up and impersonate his father and say he has to go home immediately because there's some kind of emergency?"

Zoey gave her a withering look. "That's absurd, and you know it."

Claire closed her paperback and set it down on her tray next to a barely touched plate of spaghetti. "You guys are such amateurs," she said.

Aisha was so desperate that she didn't even object to Claire's condescending tone. "Well, can *you* think of something?" she said hopefully.

"It's simple," Claire said nonchalantly. "Go to dinner with David, and over dinner casually mention that your cousin Christopher will be at the prom."

Aisha looked as if she was going to kiss Claire. "That's brilliant, Claire! That's perfect. See?" she said to Zoey. "It'll work as long as I don't let them talk to each other too much."

Zoey shook her head. "That'll never work," she said disapprovingly.

"Why not?"

"How's it going to look?" Zoey argued. "And what if either one of them tries to kiss you in front of the other?"

Aisha looked at Claire for an answer.

Claire rolled her eyes as though it was a stupid question. "Look," she said, "first of all, you can do all the slow dancing and groping and kissing with David *before* Christopher gets there."

Zoey couldn't believe she was hearing this. It was disgusting. And Aisha was eating up Claire's every word.

"And then, as soon as Christopher arrives," Claire went on, "you can take him to a more private area of the hotel for a little while. He's not going to object to that, I'm sure."

"Won't David wonder where I've gone?" Aisha asked worriedly.

"Duh," Claire said. "Just say you're going to the bathroom, and have Zoey here talk to him while you're gone."

"And if David wants to slow-dance again later in the evening?" Zoey said to Claire in a challenging tone.

"Simple," Claire answered, unfazed. "Just say your cousin's a bit overprotective."

"And what if Christopher gets a little . . . uh, overheated on the dance floor?" Zoey continued.

"Do I have to tell you *everything?*" Claire said. "Figure it out. It's not that hard . . . just say your feet hurt and you have to sit down. Jeez."

Aisha was silent for a while, as though she was going through the plan for any more possible flaws. "I don't know," she said uncertainly. "Won't David ask why Christopher doesn't have a date?"

"He's not going to notice," Claire said. "There'll be so many people there. And you can get Zoey to distract him."

Zoey kept her mouth shut.

Aisha glanced over at Zoey and bit her lip. "But what if he *does* notice?"

"Believe me," Claire said, "if you keep him happy, he won't even notice there's a band playing."

It figures Claire would think that, Zoey thought. Any guy in Claire's presence would forget his name. With a body straight out of the *Sports Illustrated* swimsuit issue and a perfect face, sometimes even women gawked. Unfortunately, actual earthlings, such as Aisha and Zoey, couldn't always count on total submission from the men around them.

Aisha seemed to be thinking along the same lines. "Claire," she said, treading carefully, "if you were there, you could pretend to be Christopher's date. That would distract him, too."

Claire was shaking her head. "No way," she said. "I'm not going."

"But it'll be fun," Aisha said, begging. "And I really need your help. Nobody can distract a guy like *you* can."

"I don't want to be anywhere near there," Claire said. "And flattery will get you nowhere."

"Please," Aisha said desperately. "I'll do anything. I can't do this on my own."

"Uh-uh," Claire said, crossing her arms in front of her, "I'm not going."

"Claire," Aisha said, "if you don't help me, the whole thing is bound to fall apart, and if that happens, so many people will be hurt. And anyway, the prom is one of the cornerstones of the high-school experience."

Claire didn't say anything, but she was still shaking her head.

"Oh, come on," Aisha continued pathetically. Her lips quivered, as if she was going to cry.

Claire sighed. "I can't stand to see you begging like that. All right, I'll go."

"Aaah," Zoey suddenly exclaimed. "I can't believe you guys are actually going to *do* this. It's crazy. And it's so . . . so deceptive."

"Precisely," Claire said smugly.

Fourteen

Ring. Ring.

Kate lifted one earphone off her ear and listened.

Ring. Ring.

She hit the stop button on her Walkman and got up from the kitchen table, where she was examining some contact prints with a magnifying glass. "Hello?"

"Kate?"

"Yes, this is she," she said. She didn't recognize the voice, but it was a woman's.

"I think you should know that Jake's involved with someone else."

Kate leaned against the kitchen counter, wondering if she was the target of some kind of practical joke. "Who is this?" she asked.

"Let's just say that I'm Jake's special friend."

The caller's speech was slightly slurred, Kate noticed. "Who is this?" she asked again, her voice rising.

"Stay away from him," the voice said ominously, "especially on prom night." Then the caller hung up.

Aisha quickly buttoned her shirt and tucked it into her jeans. She'd been concentrating so hard on her calculus homework that she'd forgotten about the time.

Zoey had invited Lucas, Aisha, and Christopher over for dinner at the Passmores' house, and Aisha was already twenty minutes late. She hurried through the kitchen and family room, then out the back door. She was running across the lawn when she heard someone calling her.

"Eesh. Wait!"

Aisha stopped and turned around. David was making his way around the house to the back door.

"Wait up, Eesh. What's your hurry?"

"I'm meeting Zoey for dinner," she explained, "and I'm really late."

"Don't you have a minute?"

"Sorry. I really can't talk now," Aisha said, moving past him. "I'll talk to you tomorrow."

"Eesh, wait," David said. "Why are you always in such a rush to get away from me? I mean, I feel like lately you're avoiding me or something."

"I'm not avoiding you," Aisha said, forcing a laugh. "I've just been so busy. You know." Aisha knew it was getting a little obvious that she had been avoiding him all week. They saw each other in calculus every morning, but every day that week she'd walked in just as the bell rang and walked out as soon as class was over. He'd barely had a chance to talk to her.

David looked at her through his tortoiseshell-rimmed glasses, as though he was trying to decide whether she was telling the truth. "Oh. Well," he said. "So where were you last night? I was here tutoring Kalif till eight-thirty, you know."

"I had to meet a friend," she said. "It was kind of important."

David's face fell, and he nodded.

"Hey," Aisha said, feeling guilty and mean, "I'll make it up to you on Saturday. Okay?"

David smiled. "Yeah. I'm really looking forward to it."

She leaned over and gave David a kiss on the cheek. "I have to go now," she said, waving and stepping backward.

"Bye," David said, a bemused look on his face.

Aisha turned around and sprinted to Zoey's house.

I'm a big jerk.

Fifteen

Benjamin took Camden Street toward the center of town. He didn't need to see in order to get around most of the island as long as he was careful to keep count of his steps. He wasn't heading for any particular place; he just needed to take a walk and get some air.

In spite of all his efforts to stop thinking about it, Nina's running away had eaten away at him all week. A huge part of it was guilt. Benjamin blamed himself for her misery even though he firmly believed that he'd done the right thing by breaking up with her. The rest of it was worry. How was Nina getting along out there? Yes, she was smart and could basically take care of herself, but Nina could also be belligerent at inappropriate times. Not every stranger was going to just let it pass. How many times had her cheekiness almost gotten her in trouble with people?

On the ferry that morning, Benjamin had spoken to Claire for a long time about whether it really was best to let Nina be. He agreed with Claire and her father on a philosophical basis, but in practical terms he wondered if it was such a good idea to let her just wander aimlessly. Claire had told him that it was his protective-boyfriend instinct kicking in, and he wondered if that was true.

Benjamin reached the circle at the center of town and sat on a bench. *How can Claire and Mr. Geiger be so passive about this?* he asked himself. *Why aren't they doing anything? Nina could get hurt.*

After a few minutes Benjamin got up. He wanted to *do* something about Nina. Anything. He didn't want to wait. They'd waited long enough. He decided to go over to the Geigers' and try to talk some sense into them. Someone had to do *something*.

Jake looked at Kate incredulously. "You're kidding," he said. "I just can't believe she would do something like that."

"It's Lara, isn't it?" Kate said.

"I'm almost a hundred percent sure it is," he said, growing more and more upset. "She's capable of just about anything."

Kate looked at him quizzically. "Jake, why did you even go out with her? She's so . . . weird."

Jake was pacing back and forth across his bedroom, his arms hanging off a baseball bat resting on his shoulders yoke style. "Because we used to hang out and get wasted together," he said matter-of-factly. "It was convenient at the time, I guess. I don't know."

Kate didn't respond but seemed to accept his explanation.

"Look," he said, stopping in front of Kate, who was sitting on the carpet and leaning against his bed. "Don't let this upset you. She's weird, but she's harmless. Okay?"

Kate nodded. "Okay . . . I guess."

Jake sensed that Kate wasn't entirely convinced. "I'll take care of it, okay?"

Kate nodded. "Yeah. Sure."

"I'll call her right now," he said, tossing the bat onto his bed. "Right now."

He grabbed the phone on his nightstand and quickly dialed Lara's phone number.

"Hello," he said gruffly after a few seconds. "Lara, it's Jake."

"Jakie!"

Jake could immediately tell that she'd been drinking, but he let it go. He had stopped trying to "save" her long ago. "Lara, did you call Kate tonight?" he asked.

Lara hiccuped. "No."

Jake felt sure she was lying, but he wanted to get a confession out of her nonetheless. "Tell me the truth, Lara," he said in a gentle voice. "I won't be angry. I promise." He gave Kate an apologetic look that he hoped communicated the reason he had to be nice to Lara.

"Hmmm, maybe," Lara said, giggling.

"Listen, Lara," Jake said. "I'm warning you to stay away from Kate. She hasn't done anything to you."

Lara was still giggling.

"If you bother her once more, I'll never speak to you again. You understand?"

Lara hiccuped again.

"Understand?"

"Yes, sir," Lara said in her deepest voice. Then she burst out laughing.

After he hung up, Jake sat next to Kate, who still seemed distressed. "Don't worry," he said reassuringly. "She's harmless."

"It's not just that, Jake," Kate said, playing with the ends of her long red hair.

"What is it?" Jake said, really wanting to set things right.

"It's this *Fatal Attraction*–type thing going on," she said, avoiding Jake's eyes. "I mean, I've told you about my experience with harassment, right?" She looked up at him, waiting for a response, a tight, rigid expression on her face.

Jake grimaced. This was definitely a delicate situation. *That* experience had ended with Kate breaking up with the guy. "Yeah," Jake said solemnly.

"I hope it doesn't happen again," Kate said resolutely.

"Oh, Kate," Jake said, trying to find the right words to set her mind at ease. "Lara's never going to harass you again. I promise."

Kate looked at Jake as though she didn't believe him. "It might be beyond your control," she said.

"No," Jake said, hurt that she didn't seem to believe him. "She won't do it again. It won't be like last time."

Kate remained silent, stubbornly refusing to give in. Jake began to feel his frustration mounting. He knew she had good reason to be nervous about the phone call, but he couldn't help but feel that she was overreacting. "Please, Kate," Jake said. "You'll see. Just give it a chance."

"I'll give it a chance, Jake," Kate said. "Because I really like you. But my tolerance for this sort of thing just isn't what it used to be."

"I understand completely," Jake said.

Would Kate give up on him just because of a jealous ex-girlfriend? he wondered. Were her feelings for him that tenuous that she'd be willing to let him go because a third party was in the way?

And then there was the matter of Kate's having gone after Benjamin first. That worried Jake, too. If she could shift her affections so easily, it made him wonder how authentic they really were. Once again he asked himself whether it was really *Jake* she was interested in, or the phantom savior from her fantasies.

* * *

"Yum," Benjamin said, sniffing the air as he followed Janelle through the foyer and into the kitchen. "Roast chicken."

Janelle laughed. "You've never been wrong yet," she said.

Claire was just getting off the phone when Benjamin walked into the kitchen.

"Portsmouth?" she was saying as Benjamin felt for a chair at the kitchen table. He knew the layout of the Geigers' house almost as well as his own, though it had been a while since he'd set foot in there.

"Hey, Benjamin just walked in," she said. "So I'd better go. Thanks again for the info."

Benjamin heard her slippers slap against the tiled floor as she crossed the room to put the phone back in its cradle. "Who was that?" he asked.

"That was Zoey," Claire said, coming back toward him. Benjamin could tell something was up just by Claire's intonation. He also knew there was no love lost between Claire and his sister, so neither one of them would call the other just to chat.

"And?" he prodded as Claire took a seat across from him.

"She was at the restaurant with Lara," Claire said, "and Lara got a call from a friend of hers in Kittery who says she met a Nina *Temple* from Chatham Island."

"Really?" Benjamin said. "Nina Temple?"

"Yeah. She had bright red hair."

"Same one, for sure."

"They met on a bus to Portsmouth, New Hampshire."

"How long ago was this?" Benjamin asked.

"Lara's friend got off at Kittery at about five-thirty yesterday."

"So," Benjamin said, doing the math in his head,

117

"Nina got into Portsmouth about twenty-four hours ago, right?"

Claire didn't answer, but Benjamin imagined she was nodding.

"So what are you going to do about it?" he asked. "Does your dad know?"

"No," Claire said. "I just got the call from Zoey two seconds ago. And my dad won't be back until late. He's taken Sarah dearest out to dinner in Weymouth."

"Can't you get him on his cell phone?" Benjamin suggested. "I mean, don't you think you should tell him?"

"Nah," Claire said dismissively. "I don't want to interrupt his dinner. Even if it *is* with the midget."

"Claire!" Benjamin said, shocked. "How can you be so calm? Don't you even care what happens to your sister?" He was all riled up and he was yelling, but he didn't care. Nina's life was at stake.

"Get a grip, Benjamin," she said. "Nina's fine. She called just before Zoey."

"She did?" Benjamin felt at once excited and relieved. "What did she say? Where is she?"

"She wouldn't tell me where she was," Claire said. "But she said she's fine. Nothing bad has happened to her. So relax."

Benjamin took a deep breath. Nina was probably still in Portsmouth, which wasn't that far away. . . .

"Call your dad, Claire," Benjamin ordered.

"No." Claire sounded as if she thought he was crazy.

"Come on, Claire," Benjamin said impatiently. "He'll want to go after her when he finds out she's in Portsmouth."

"No," Claire said. "My dad gave Nina his word. He promised not to go after her."

Benjamin screwed up his mouth and clenched his hands into fists in an effort not to explode. "Claire," he said in a tight voice, "Nina could get into serious trouble. In fact, we're lucky that she's still okay after wandering around for four days." He paused, breathing heavily in anger. "Now, are you going to do something about it or not?"

"I guess I'm going to have to say *not*," Claire responded evenly. "Would you like to stay for dinner, by the way?"

Benjamin couldn't believe his ears. He knew Claire could be coldhearted and manipulative, but he had never expected her to be this unfeeling toward her own sister. It made him sick to think he had actually been in love with Claire at one time. No wonder Nina was so insecure—and no wonder she'd left.

Benjamin stood up abruptly. "You can sit here passively if you want to, Claire—but *I'm* going after her."

After Benjamin had stormed out of the house, Claire sat at the kitchen table to have some of Janelle's roast chicken. She smiled to herself. *God, I'm good. In fact, I'm amazing.* Even Benjamin, who was nearly impossible to manipulate, had fallen for her tricks. It hadn't even been difficult, because he was still madly in love with Nina. Claire only had to help bring it out. She laughed, thinking about how uncharacteristically out-of-control he had been. How *emotional*.

Claire played out the rest of the story in her head: Benjamin would go after Nina, and the closer he got to finding her, the more he would realize that he loved her. By the time he found her (and even if he didn't), the passion in their relationship would be restored, and in the end, both Nina and Benjamin would be happy. It was perfect.

Sixteen

"Zoey, *really*," Claire said, laughing hysterically. "Tina and Benny?" She glanced down at the student-run literary magazine again. "Ooh! This is my favorite part," she said, giggling. "'She had sung her delightful tunes while playing the pianoforte.'" Claire tried to stifle her laughter. "Just picture it," she said, trying to speak through her laughter. "Can you imagine Nina singing at the pianoforte?"

Aisha had tears of laughter streaming down her face. "I think it's rather brilliant," she said in her best English accent. "I didn't know our friend was so *clevah*."

"Ha, ha, you guys," Zoey said sorely. "I'm glad you're so amused." She looked away from her so-called friends, completely humiliated and hurt that they thought the story was so funny. When she'd written it, she hadn't meant it to be humorous.

She scanned the cafeteria for Lucas one more time. Lunchtime was almost over, and he hadn't shown his face yet. He was probably afraid to face her, Zoey thought. And he should be. The jerk.

Zoey hadn't even noticed that her notebook was missing from her bedroom, so there was no way she could have stopped Lucas from submitting her piece to the literary magazine, which had run it as part of their

120

occasional series entitled "Parodies of Great Literature." Now it had been published in *Folio,* an eight-page photocopied pamphlet distributed monthly among the student body and faculty, and she had all of Weymouth High rolling with laughter whether she liked it or not.

Lucas suddenly burst in through one of the swinging doors and went straight to the food line.

Zoey grabbed the magazine from Claire's hand and marched over to him. "You'd better have something to say about this!" she yelled from ten feet away, waving it in the air.

Lucas spun around and automatically raised his arms in self-defense.

"You had no business showing my story to anyone!" she said furiously. "You had no business reading it yourself!"

"Don't be mad," Lucas said, abandoning his tray and coming over to face her. "Please, Zoey. I—"

Zoey threw the magazine at him, and the pages scattered to the floor. "You *what,* Lucas? What possible explanation can you have for invading my privacy for the third time in two weeks?" she said, shaking with fury.

"You were going to show it to me, remember?" he said weakly.

"Are you really that dumb?" Zoey asked. "Or are you just trying to get out of this?"

Lucas looked at her, speechless. He was turning red, and the whole cafeteria was watching them. Zoey didn't care. The whole school already thought she was an idiot, anyway. "I just can't believe you would do this!" she said angrily. "What were you *thinking?*"

"I thought it was really good," Lucas managed to say. "God, Zoey. It's so funny."

Zoey clenched her jaw and glared at him. "What does *that* have to do with anything?"

"Oh, come on, Zo," he said imploringly. "I didn't do it to piss you off."

"Then *why*," she said, balling her hands into fists, "did you do it?"

"Because I was really impressed," he said, "and I knew you'd never agree to send it into the magazine."

"That's my decision," Zoey snapped, "not yours."

"But you thought it was silly," Lucas explained, "and I figured that after everyone told you how funny it was, maybe you'd realize that you're really talented."

"You know, Lucas," Zoey said, her hands on her hips, "I don't think you have a friggin' brain in that pointed head of yours."

Lucas winced. "Zo, you should be proud of your writing. It's great. You make people laugh."

Zoey made a guttural sound. "I don't ever, *ever* want to look at you or speak to you again, you slime."

"But Zo—"

"Just shut up and leave me alone," she said, turning to leave.

"Does this mean you don't want to go to the prom anymore?" Zoey heard him say behind her.

"The prom?" Zoey said, spinning around to look at him. "You're so lame. I wouldn't even go to . . . to . . . to Paris with you if you handed me a first-class ticket! Forget the stupid prom."

Zoey picked up her book bag and stomped out of the cafeteria. *Weasel. Scum. Dolt. Creep.*

She felt her eyes brimming with tears. She had meant the story to be serious.

Benjamin carefully tapped directly in front of him with his white cane. He was crossing a street and had begun to feel the road dip slightly, which meant he was approaching the curb. Once the stick made contact with the curb, he carefully stepped up and silently added it to the count in his head. Four blocks behind him, two to go.

He had been feeling his way around Portsmouth all afternoon, and he was beginning to feel the mental strain. This was the first time Benjamin had visited an entirely new city without anyone to guide him, and though it was slightly unnerving, he found it to be sort of stimulating, too. All his senses seemed to be sharpening, and he was beginning to detect even the most subtle sounds and movements around him.

From the bus station, Benjamin had taken a cab to the nearest travel agency, where he had asked for a list of phone numbers for all local hotels in the low- to medium-priced range. The woman who had helped him was extraordinarily accommodating and quickly put together the list especially for him. Benjamin had long ago learned to cope with the special treatment most people gave him when they realized he was blind, and though he still resented being pitied, he also appreciated the occasional perks: faster service, greater courtesy, and more attention in general.

Zoey had tried to stop him from leaving when she caught him packing a bag that morning, and when she realized he was unstoppable, she had offered to go with him. But for some reason Benjamin felt strongly that he had to do this on his own. He saw the expedition as a sort of preparation for going to college at Columbia University, which would be an even bigger challenge. In a few months, Benjamin would be heading out *by himself* into New York, perhaps the most volatile and exciting city in the world, and he felt that now was the time to start learning to be more self-sufficient.

When Benjamin reached the sixth block, he walked several more paces, then stopped where he thought the hotel might be located. He waited until he heard someone approaching, then prepared himself for the most humiliating part.

"Excuse me," he said. "I'm blind, and I need to find the Castle Inn. Would you mind pointing me in the right direction?"

A young boy's voice answered him. "No problem," he said, "it's right over there."

"Could you help me out a little more than that?" Benjamin said patiently. "Like, maybe you could tell me if I'm standing right in front of it?"

"Oh, sure," the boy said. He was probably about ten, Benjamin guessed. "I'll take you there." He took Benjamin by the arm and walked him about twenty steps. "Okay, we're right outside the front door."

"Thanks," Benjamin said, tapping the pavement to find the step.

"Bye," the boy said, leaving Benjamin to fend for himself.

Once he was in the lobby, Benjamin took a moment to orient himself, concentrating on the sounds and smells around him. Musty old carpeting. Piped-in Barbra Streisand. Young male connecting a phone call to one of the rooms. Female attending to a guest at the reception desk directly in front of him, about fifteen feet away. Someone smoking a cigarette, probably waiting for someone. Coffee shop to his left. It was the most stimulation he'd been exposed to in a long, long time, and it felt good. Even when he'd been in Miami over spring break with the rest of the gang, Benjamin hadn't felt this alive. He had spent most of that trip avoiding Nina and listening to the radio in his hotel room.

He stepped up to the front desk and paid for a room. Then he asked the woman if she would help him by reading off the first two phone numbers on his list of hotels. Benjamin memorized them, then asked her if there was a pay phone in the lobby. She showed him the phone booth and told him she'd be around if he needed anything else.

"Thanks for your help," Benjamin said as he put down his small overnight bag and found the seat in the booth. He dialed the first number.

"Hello?" Benjamin said, hope rising inside him. "I'd like to know if a Nina Geiger is registered in your hotel. . . ."

From the widow's walk, Claire and Aaron had a clear view of Coast Road. They'd been watching for Claire's father's Mercedes for the last forty minutes while Sarah waited downstairs in the living room, absolutely livid.

As planned, Aaron had taken his mother out for a pleasant Saturday morning drive around Chatham Island. Sarah had been feeling chipper when she left the house, but according to Aaron, her mood had shifted dramatically as soon as she spotted two Mercedeses parked next to each other, and then Burke Geiger holding Jordan Kestler by the hand as Jordan was stepping over a fallen tree by the lake. Sarah had demanded that Aaron stop the car, but Aaron refused, explaining to her that it was always a bad idea to leap to conclusions. It would be embarrassing for all four of them if she made false accusations, he'd told her. From there Aaron had taken her back to the Geigers', where she'd been stewing and muttering under her breath ever since.

"Look. He's coming!" Claire said, so excited that

she could hardly keep herself from jumping up and down.

Aaron laughed. "I don't think I've ever seen you this happy before, Claire. We should ruin people's lives more often."

Claire felt prematurely triumphant. She'd been trying to break up Sarah and her father for so long that even Aaron couldn't dampen her spirits. "Come on," she said. "We'd better go downstairs. We don't want to miss *this* show."

They went down into the second-floor guest bedroom and waited until they heard Claire's father come in through the kitchen from the garage. But before they realized he was even in the house, they heard Sarah's voice. "Burke, where were you just now?" she said with remarkable calm.

It sounded as if they were in the kitchen, Claire thought. Fortunately for Janelle, it was her day off.

Claire and Aaron slipped out of the guest room and crouched down at the top of the staircase. They couldn't see into the kitchen, but the voices were loud and clear.

"I told you, sweetie," Claire's father answered. "I had a meeting this morning."

"Liar," Sarah said venomously.

"Sarah," he said, "what's the matter?"

"Tell me the truth, Burke," she said. "At least respect me enough to do that."

"I *am* telling you the truth," he said. "I was at a meeting about a new property I'm thinking of acquiring."

"Jesus—I can't believe you can look me straight in the eye and tell me lies." A sob. "First the letter, now this," she said, her voice cracking. "Is it the same woman? Is it *Madeline?*"

126

"Sarah, what is going on?"

"I saw you, Burke. I saw the whole thing."

"What?" he said, raising his voice in frustration. "What did you see?"

Sarah made a grunting sound. "Don't even try to pretend."

"Sarah," Claire's father said reasonably, "I was looking at some land over by Big Bite Pond. Have I done something to upset you?"

Claire's heart lurched as she heard her father's voice catch in his throat. His tone was filled with anger, confusion, and disappointment.

"Who was that woman?" Sarah asked, enunciating every syllable.

Claire's father didn't answer right away. He was probably struggling to figure out what woman she was talking about. "Who? . . . Oh, you must have seen me talking to Jordan Kestler. She owns the land. My meeting was with her."

"And do you normally hold hands with all your business associates?" Sarah said sarcastically.

"Hold hands? *What?*"

Sarah was sobbing now, and it was a while before she said anything more. "That's a likely story," she finally said. "I believe *that* about as much as I believe that you don't know Madeline."

"It's true!" he said. He was speaking more quietly now. "Both those things are true."

Claire heard Sarah passing through the foyer and into the living room, and then she heard her father follow her.

"Burke, this is the last straw," Sarah said with finality. "I will not stand for this kind of abuse."

"But I'm telling you the truth. I love you, Sarah. Only you."

Once again there was silence. Claire pictured her father pacing back and forth across the living room.

"Forget it," Sarah said. "It's over. Aaron will help me pack my things this afternoon." She paused, and Claire guessed she was probably trying to contain another wave of tears. "I've decided to move back into my apartment in Weymouth."

"For good?"

"Yes, Burke. For good," Sarah said in a barely audible voice. "I've seen a side of you that I just can't accept—that I loathe. I can't marry you now."

"Aren't you even going to consider that you might be wrong?" Claire's father pleaded.

"No," she said. "I've seen all I need to see."

No one said anything, and Claire suddenly became aware of Aaron's breath on her cheek.

"Please tell Aaron I've gone for a walk and that I'll be back in an hour," she said in a choked voice.

The front door opened, then slammed shut. For a moment Claire felt a stunning wave of grief. But this was what she'd wanted, wasn't it? Claire turned around and looked at Aaron. His face was two inches away from hers, and she could see vulnerability in his tender expression. Seeing his mother so upset had cut right into him, Claire guessed. And he was probably sorry that he ever agreed to be a party to Claire's scheme.

Without thinking, Claire put her lips to his and kissed him softly.

Prom Countdown

2:00 P.M.

Claire and Aisha revise and perfect the prom plan and go over it again and again.

3:22 P.M.

Zoey writes in her journal. She can't believe that the night she's been looking forward to forever is going to suck, thanks to Lucas.

3:30 P.M.

Aisha is a nervous wreck. She's really sorry she let her two-timing get this far. She takes a hot shower to calm herself.

3:42 P.M.

Kate is looking forward to the prom like nothing before. She is standing in front of the mirror, admiring how great she looks in her emerald green minidress. She's tried it on seven times already.

3:50 P.M.

Claire wonders what she should wear to the prom. She opens her closet and pulls out a selection of formal dresses, then decides to take a nap and worry about it later.

3:55 P.M.

Zoey goes down to the kitchen and sneaks a peek out the window at the Cabrals' house, hoping to catch Lucas looking sorry and miserable.

4:05 P.M.

Aisha binges on a pint of Häagen-Dazs and a box of Oreos, thinking over and over, *What if something goes wrong tonight?*

4:24 P.M.

Kate tries on another shade of lipstick and pictures how handsome Jake will look in a tuxedo. It's going to be the best night of her life. Even Lara's threats can't dampen her spirits.

4:30 P.M.

Claire wakes up with her pulse racing. She's just had a dream in which she's kissing Aaron passionately in a hotel room.

4:43 P.M.

A button pops off Aisha's red crepe dress as she's

130

putting it on. She sees it as an omen: Her life is *definitely* going to fall apart that night.

4:48 P.M.

Lara arrives at the Passmores' house. She promised to help out at the restaurant, and Mr. Passmore asked her to pick something up at the house before coming over.

4:51 P.M.

Kate puts on the final touches of makeup and slips out of her robe. A fingernail catches on her stockings, creating a huge, irreparable run.

4:52 P.M.

Lara overhears Zoey talking to Kate on the phone. Kate is coming over to borrow a pair of stockings.

4:55 P.M.

Zoey goes down to the kitchen and sneaks another peek at the Cabrals' house, hoping to catch Lucas looking sorry and miserable.

4:58 P.M.

Lara watches as Kate pulls up in the Cabrals' car.

4:59 P.M.

Lucas stares at his phone, wondering if he should call Zoey and try to apologize. Christopher reports to work at Mi Piace.

5:00 P.M.

Jake runs out of his AA meeting, and heads for the locker room, where he's going to get ready for a great night.

5:05 P.M.

Kate leaves the Passmores' in a pair of Mrs. Passmore's sheer black stockings.

5:06 P.M.

Lara takes the Passmores' car keys, which are hanging on the magnetic hook stuck to the refrigerator.

5:15 P.M.

Claire starts thinking about how Aisha can repay her for posing as Christopher's date for the evening.

5:30 P.M.

Jake watches as the ferry approaches Weymouth.

5:40 P.M.

David and Aisha get into a stretch limousine in Weymouth and head for Le Souffle.

6:00 P.M.

Claire presses the long black body-hugging dress she's decided to wear. She feels relieved that she and

Aaron finally succeeded in breaking up their folks—
but she also feels oddly empty.

6:10 P.M.

Zoey gets in the shower.

6:25 P.M.

Lucas gets in the shower.

7:00 P.M.

David and Aisha watch as the waiter prepares crêpes
Suzette for two on a rolling table.

7:14 P.M.

David takes Aisha around his neighborhood in the
limo. They stop at a huge park and take a romantic
walk on one of the footpaths.

7:22 P.M.

Zoey forces herself to put on her dress, a chic mid-
calf-length dress in navy, which she suddenly hates.
She contemplates not going at all.

7:26 P.M.

Sitting on a park bench, David kisses Aisha.

7:34 P.M.

Aisha momentarily stops kissing David. She feels
light-headed from lack of oxygen.

7:40 P.M.

The ferry pulls out of Chatham Island. Lucas, Zoey, and Claire are all on board, but they're not talking to one another.

8:06 P.M.

Aisha and David arrive at the Ambassador Hotel. Aisha feels really cool driving up in a limo.

8:10 P.M.

Zoey, Lucas, and Claire walk into the grand ballroom at the Ambassador Hotel.

Seventeen

Kate slipped off her brand-new high-heeled sandals and dumped them in the passenger side of the Cabrals' beat-up Toyota. Having had to stop by Zoey's to replace her ruined stockings, there was no way she could have caught the 5:10 ferry on foot, even though it was only two blocks away, so she'd borrowed the Cabrals' car.

With only two minutes to spare, Kate nervously stuck the key into the ignition and started the car. She was sweating profusely from having run around like a maniac, and she didn't have the time to stop and fix her makeup. If there was one thing she hated about living on the island, it was the rigid ferry schedule. If she missed it, she would have had to shell out major bucks to catch a water taxi, because Jake would be waiting for her in Weymouth and the next ferry wasn't for another two and a half hours.

She took a deep breath when she stopped at the intersection of Camden and South Streets. "Relax. You'll make it," she said to herself as she checked to make sure the road was clear before turning.

She took a left onto South Street and adjusted the rearview mirror. She noticed that her mascara was already running—and that there was a familiar blue

Honda about two car lengths behind her. Wasn't that the Passmores' car? she wondered.

She felt a sudden jolt and quickly looked over her shoulder. The blue car had bumped into her and was right on her tail. Kate stepped on the gas, and her car lurched forward. She glanced into the rearview mirror again and tried to identify the driver in the other car.

Oh, my God. It's Lara, she realized with horror. Panicking, Kate accelerated just as she reached the very end of South Street. She veered to the right, onto Dock Street, but as she did, Lara rammed into her again—harder this time—and Kate's car spun off the road and into a narrow ditch that separated the beach area from the street.

Kate felt a sharp stab of pain on her forehead, then everything went black.

Jake leaned over the railing as the ferry came into view. He shielded his eyes from the glare of the late afternoon sun, and watched as the vessel sent ripples across the glimmering surface of the water.

He tried to imagine what Kate would look like when she stepped off the ferry in the emerald green dress . . . her soft red hair cascading down her back . . . the freckled skin on her perfectly sculpted shoulders . . . her long, graceful arms . . . her slim, shapely legs . . . God, she was so painfully beautiful.

Jake still doubted her feelings for him, but he couldn't stop himself from feeling more and more for *her*. As he was getting ready for the prom earlier, he had promised himself that he would do everything in his power to make it the best night of her life, and in that way, he hoped, she would forget about the man in her dreams and fall unequivocally in love with *him*, Jake McRoyan.

In his hand Jake held a single white orchid carefully

arranged with some ferns. He'd spent a good part of the morning looking for the perfect corsage to present to her, and when he saw it, he knew it was just right: an orchid's delicate beauty belied its sturdiness and strength. Just like Kate.

The ferry was docking now, its whistle loud and shrill, and Jake began nervously fiddling with his bow tie and cummerbund. He scanned the upper deck, hoping to find her waving down at him, but he couldn't see her. Then he peered into the covered cabin on the lower level, where he spotted Aisha—but he couldn't find Kate among all the other passengers.

The gangway was lowered and the ropes were tied, and the passengers began to file out, spilling out onto the landing. Jake stretched up on tiptoe, his rented tuxedo shirt slipping out from under his black cummerbund. He was looking for her red hair or a spot of green. Within a minute, all the passengers had disembarked, leaving only the captain and a deckhand on board.

Jake searched the landing, taking in the scattering of individuals who had just stepped off the ferry. Where was she? He had a sudden urge to run up to Aisha and ask if she'd seen Kate, but instead he watched as the ferry slowly chugged out into the calm gray depths of the sound. He watched as it grew smaller and smaller, a jumble of emotions fighting its way to the surface of his subconscious.

Then, all at once, the realization hit him with tremendous force. She hadn't come. She'd blown him off. She'd finally realized what Jake had known all along: She was not in love with Jake but with some figment of her imagination, a romantic illusion.

Jake closed his eyes and pictured her beautiful face, savoring the image for the last time. Then he crushed the white orchid in his hand and threw it into the water.

Eighteen

Thank God we're finally here, Lucas thought as he, Zoey, and Claire walked toward the ballroom. The ferry and taxi rides over from Chatham Island had been sheer torture, with hardly a word spoken among them. Lucas had tried to be nice to Zoey, making small talk with her, telling her how beautiful she looked. He'd even given her a rose corsage, which she'd refused to accept, and told her about two hundred times how sorry he was about submitting her story to the literary review. By the time they got to the Ambassador Hotel, Lucas had just about given up, and he resigned himself to spending the rest of the evening alone.

Lucas could hear the band playing a really danceable song by the Gypsy Kings as the three of them handed over their tickets to one of the organizers, who was standing outside the ballroom. And as soon as the doors opened, the music blasted out full force, giving Lucas his first taste of the spirited party going on inside.

"See you later, *Claire,*" Zoey said as soon as she walked in, pointedly ignoring Lucas. She left to join a group of girls from her French class.

Claire waved hello to Aisha, who was already tearing up the dance floor with the guy she had kissed at Louise Kronenberger's house. Lucas quickly averted his glance. Whatever Aisha was up to, he didn't want to know. Christopher was arriving at about ten, and Lucas didn't want to see anything he would feel compelled to tell Christopher about later. As far as he was concerned, it was none of his business.

Now the band was playing the theme song from the movie *Dangerous Minds,* and most of the people cleared off the dance floor. Lucas checked his watch. Where were Jake and Kate? he wondered. He figured they would have already arrived.

One of Claire's many admirers came up to talk to her, so Lucas made his way over to the buffet table. Claire could certainly take care of herself.

He picked up a plate and some silverware and began working his way down the table. Cold cuts, baked clams, veal Milanese, chicken teriyaki, buffalo wings, pasta primavera, and a whole separate table of fruit and pastries. Not a bad spread, he thought, loading up his plate.

He turned around when he heard overly zealous giggling. Unmistakably Zoey's giggling. She was talking to some dweeb Lucas recognized but couldn't quite place, and, annoyingly, she looked like she was having the time of her life. He turned back to the food table, convincing himself that it was nothing to get upset about. Zoey was friendly with so many people at school. She'd always been popular and well liked.

Just as Lucas reached the end of the buffet, Zoey and the dweeb came over to the table.

"Oh, so much food!" she said as though Lucas weren't there. "And everything looks so good." She picked up two plates and handed one to the dweeb.

"Thanks," the dweeb said, giving her a fake, flirty smile.

"I wasn't really hungry yet," Zoey said to him. "But

139

just looking at all this delicious food whets my appetite."

The dweeb smiled (again, fake and flirty). "Here, let me help you with that," he said, taking Zoey's small beaded evening bag from her.

Zoey giggled, though Lucas failed to see what was so funny. "Oh, thanks," she said. "That's much better . . . oh, but now you don't have any hands free."

Zoey and the dweeb sat down at one of the many round tables scattered around the dance floor. They were partially hidden from Lucas's view because of the enormous floral centerpiece, so Lucas discreetly moved a few paces to the left, careful to take only barely discernible baby steps.

Over the loud music, Lucas couldn't hear a thing they were saying, so instead he made a quick assessment of their body language. Zoey's posture was open and friendly and approachable; the dweeb's was aggressive, leering, and potentially dangerous. Lucas decided to keep an eye on them, just in case the dweeb made any suspicious moves.

A slow tune came on, and Aisha pulled the spin-the-bottle guy onto the dance floor. Several feet away from her, Claire was shaking her head, refusing to dance with a forlorn-looking guy. Then the dweeb started to get up from his seat. *You'd better be going to the bathroom,* Lucas mentally addressed the dweeb, *because if you're thinking what I think you're thinking . . .*

Then Zoey started getting up. And before he knew what he was doing, Lucas dropped his plate onto the nearest table and lunged after them. But in the process he tripped over a chair, pulling the tablecloth and the centerpiece down with him. There was a loud crash, and several people stopped to stare at him. Thankfully, the band kept right on playing.

From a distance Zoey gave him a cold stare and angrily said something Lucas couldn't hear over the music. It looked a lot like "Stay away from me." Then she spun around and marched off to the dance floor with the dweeb in tow.

Christopher checked his watch as he strode confidently into the ballroom. 9:50. Ten minutes earlier than he'd expected. He quickly scanned the room for Aisha. At least four hundred seniors were in the room, he estimated, the guys decked out in their tuxedos, the girls all made up and in their formal dresses. About fifty round tables, with huge flower arrangements, were positioned all over the vast room. A six-piece band. It was pretty impressive.

"Christopher!"

With a huge grin, Aisha suddenly emerged from the mass of bodies. She was wearing a dramatic deep red dress and she looked flushed and excited. Christopher couldn't help but gawk. He'd never seen her in such a low-cut, daring outfit before. She looked fabulous.

"You're stunning," he said to her breathlessly.

Aisha laughed. "Thanks," she said, kissing him on the cheek. "Want to go for a walk?"

"But I just got here."

"And I've been here for hours," she said. She slipped her arm around his waist. "Let's go get some air." She winked at him suggestively.

Christopher raised his eyebrows in surprise but let her steer him back out the door, down a long hallway, past a cocktail lounge, and through glass double doors. Where was she taking him? he wondered, his excitement building. She led him through another set of glass doors to the outside, and a kidney-shaped pool, all lit up by underwater lamps, came into view. Around the pool were white

141

lounge chairs, little tables, and bigger ones with closed beach umbrellas protruding from their centers.

"Now, isn't it better out here, away from all those people?" she said, pulling him down onto one of the lounge chairs.

Christopher leaned toward her, forcing her to recline. "Much better," he said. "Much, much better."

He brought his face to hers and kissed her warm, full lips. Her arms wrapped around his back, instantly relaxing his taut muscles. Christopher ran a hand over her bare back, savoring the smoothness of her skin.

He planted small kisses, first on her eyes, then on each cheek, then her chin, her neck, her collarbone . . .

"Excuse me," Claire said to Tommy Wilkins, who had been regaling her with stories about snowboarding for the last fifteen minutes. "I have to go talk to my friend right now."

"Well, hurry back," he said, winking. "I'll be right over there." He pointed to a table of his buddies.

"Right," Claire said as she turned away.

Aisha and Christopher were standing at the main doors to the ballroom. By the smile on Christopher's face and the way his eyes seemed to be picking up every detail, Claire could tell that he was enjoying the spectacle. He looked dapper in his tuxedo; meanwhile, Aisha's lipstick was smeared, and she badly needed to run a comb through her hair.

"Hi," Claire said, approaching them. She put on her brightest smile and sidled up to Christopher. "How was the restaurant opening?" she asked him.

Christopher looked at Claire closely. "Oh, fine," he said after a moment's hesitation.

"Really?" Claire said, motioning behind his back for Aisha to go.

"Well, actually," Christopher said, "it was kind of a disaster. Everything that could have gone wrong did."

"Um, Christopher," Aisha said nervously, "I have to go to the bathroom for a sec. I'll be back."

Christopher nodded. "Okay, we'll wait for you here."

"Hmmm. Maybe we should wait over there instead," Claire said, gently steering Christopher to a table far away from where David was sitting.

"So, do you think the restaurant's going to be a success?" Claire asked as she slipped into a seat next to Christopher.

"Oh, I think so." He nodded. "The food's pretty good, and the place is done up really nicely."

"Not to mention that there aren't many other restaurants on the island," Claire added.

"Yeah. That too."

Claire managed to keep the conversation going until Aisha got back. In fact, she had Christopher so charmed that he didn't even seem to notice that Aisha was gone for a full fifteen minutes.

"I'm back," Aisha announced. Her hair was still a mess, Claire noted, and now her lipstick was all gone. Claire didn't even want to think about how the rest of it had come off. The thought of tongue-wrestling two guys, one after the other . . . *yuck*.

Claire excused herself as Aisha took her seat. Already Aisha was feeling the strain of having to divide herself between two dates, and there was still a long night ahead. David had been worried that Aisha was gone so long (making out with Christopher had taken a half hour), and so Aisha had promised not to stay away too long this time. She could probably get away with ten minutes, she figured, before David started getting worried again.

143

"Eesh, why do you keep looking at your watch?" Christopher asked, sounding half amused.

"Oh! Was I?" Aisha said guiltily. "Gee, I don't know. Habit, I guess."

"Well, relax," he said. "We're supposed to be having fun. And this is a great party."

"I'm *having* fun," Aisha said defensively. "Hey, it's my prom."

The dance floor began to fill up as the band started playing "My Sharona." "You want to dance?" Christopher said, getting up and holding out his hand. "This song's a classic."

"Oh, no!" Aisha said, leaping out of her seat. "You know what? I forgot my purse at the other—I mean, in the bathroom. I have to go get it." She gave him an apologetic look, praying that Claire would show up soon.

"It's okay," Christopher said. "I'll wait."

"I'll be two seconds. I promise."

"Yeah. Okay."

"No longer than that," Aisha said, stalling.

"Okay," Christopher said, shooing her away with hand gestures. "Go. What are you waiting for?"

Aisha bent over and pretended to adjust one of the straps on her shoes. Where was Claire?

"Eesh, what are you doing under the tablecloth?"

It was Claire's voice. *Thank you, God,* Aisha said to herself. "Oh, you know," Aisha said, pulling herself upright, "new shoes."

"Did you know this hotel had a spa?" Claire said, smoothly distracting Christopher. "I saw a sign in the lobby. It looks fabulous."

"I'll be right back," Aisha said, squeezing Christopher's shoulder. "I just have to get my purse," she said to Claire, giving her a meaningful look.

144

Aisha quickly walked over to David's table, glancing over her shoulder to make sure that Christopher wasn't watching. The plan seemed to be working so far, but Aisha swore to herself that she would never attempt anything like it ever again. It was just too nerve-racking and dangerous. If she got caught . . . she didn't even want to think about what would happen if either one of the guys caught on.

David was talking to two seniors when Aisha arrived at his side. "Hey, Eesh," David said. "You know Dan and Christine, don't you?"

"Yes, of course," Aisha said, greeting them with a warm smile.

"Why don't you sit down?" David said, pulling her by the hand. "We were just talking about—what else—college." He laughed lightly.

Aisha looked at the group uneasily. "I have—"

"Christine's going to Barnard in the fall," David went on. "Isn't that cool? It's supposed to be one of the hippest colleges in the country."

"David, uh—" Aisha said, leaning forward to speak into his ear.

"Yeah?" he said, uncrossing his legs and giving her his full attention.

"I just ran into my cousin," Aisha lied. She was trying to make herself sound surprised and excited by the coincidence, but somehow the words just wouldn't come out right.

"Your cousin?"

"Yeah, uh, he came as someone's date," Aisha explained. "Actually, you met her."

"Who?"

"Claire Geiger," Aisha said, smiling apologetically at Dan and Christine for interrupting their conversation.

"Claire?"

"Yeah. You know, the really pretty, well-endowed one you met at Louise's house."

"Oh, right," David said, moving his head up and down. "I remember her."

"Anyway," Aisha said, semi-squatting to be at David's eye level, "she's with my cousin, and I promised that I'd dance a couple of songs with him." Aisha hated the way she sounded. The lines seemed so rehearsed and fake. "You don't mind, do you?"

"No, no," David said, shaking his head. "Why should I mind if you want to dance with your cousin? In fact, why don't you bring him by afterward so I can meet him?"

"Yeah, okay, sure," Aisha said uncertainly. "See you in a few minutes."

Aisha went back to Christopher and Claire's table, her purse tucked under her arm. Three other couples had now joined the table, but Claire and Christopher were keeping to themselves, talking to each other quietly. Aisha silently thanked Claire for holding up her end of the deal. She really was a master when it came to distracting men. "Hi again," Aisha said just as the band broke into the twist-contest song from *Pulp Fiction*.

"Hey!" Christopher said. "Ready for a dance?"

Aisha carefully put her purse down on the table. "Mind if I borrow him for a minute?" she asked Claire.

"Be my guest," Claire said good-naturedly. "He's all yours."

Aisha took Christopher's hand as he led her onto the dance floor. He tried to pull her to an area that was less crowded, and that would therefore make them more conspicuous, but Aisha pulled back. "No!" she yelled over the blare of the music. "Let's just stay near our table. I have to keep an eye on my purse."

146

Christopher shook his head in bewilderment, but he seemed to accept her excuse. "Fine with me!" he shouted back as he started to dance, twisting easily to the music. Aisha tried to follow his movements, but she was reasonably sure that it looked more like she was writhing in pain than doing the twist. He moved fluidly, effortlessly, instinctively. Meanwhile she had to think really hard about which limb to move next. Even in the best of circumstances, dancing was not her forte. But now, when she was tense, it was almost impossible to listen for the beat.

"Wild Thing" was the next song, but Aisha was pooped, and all she wanted to do was sit down. She moved close to Christopher to tell him that she'd had enough, but before she knew it, he had both arms wrapped around her and was dragging her to the center of the dance floor. "I'm having a great time, Eesh," he said. "Thanks for inviting me."

Out of the corner of her eye Aisha could see David's table, which meant he could see her, too. "I really need to sit down, Christopher," she said. "That twist thing really took a lot out of me."

Christopher grinned. "You're out of shape," he said, laughing. "Or maybe you just need some inspiration."

Oh, no, Aisha thought, watching his lips come closer in what seemed like slow motion. *He's going to kiss me!*

Christopher gently pressed Aisha's body closer to his.

Stop! Aisha was yelling in her mind. *David might see.* "Christo—"

His lips were on hers the next second. Aisha was totally and completely helpless.

Nineteen

Claire smiled to herself as she watched Aisha struggle through the twist. She was hopeless, an antidote to the stereotype that all black people were good dancers. But Christopher looked pretty good out there. He could *definitely* move.

Claire's eyes lingered on them a while longer, then she shifted her gaze to the band. They'd been doing a decent job all night. They had a lot of energy, and their repertoire was remarkably varied. All in all, Claire thought, the prom was a success. And everyone seemed to be having a good time; everyone except Claire, that is.

She'd agreed to come only because Aisha so desperately needed her help, and because it seemed that a good ploy like Aisha's was just what Claire needed to distract her from thinking about Nina and Aaron and Sarah Mendel.

Proms were more Nina's sort of thing, she realized. Nina would have made a million jokes about the whole event, but she would relish being here with her friends and partying. Claire suddenly realized that part of the cause for the gnawing feeling in her chest was that she missed her sister. And maybe part of it was guilt about intentionally causing her father so much misery. But there was something else, too. She couldn't quite put her finger on it.

Then the band moved into a slow song, and Claire suddenly realized why she was in a funk. It was because no matter how hard she'd tried to get over him, she still felt something for Aaron. She'd kissed him that morning before she could stop herself—and it had been *so* sweet. Claire had immediately felt close to him, connected in some fundamental yet inexplicable way. She had never felt that for anyone before, and if she was totally honest with herself, she was afraid that she never would again.

"Claire?"

Claire blinked and looked up. Aaron was standing right next to her, holding a single long-stemmed red rose. "Aaron," Claire said, feeling strange and floaty, as if she were in a dream.

"Claire, will you dance with me?" he said humbly, almost shyly.

Without speaking, Claire took the rose from his hand, then slowly stood up. She looked into his eyes and felt a powerful rush of emotion. He took her by the hand and led her to a corner of the dance floor.

The feel of Aaron's cheek against hers was incredible—warm and soft and comforting—but after a moment Aaron pulled back to gaze into her eyes. Claire felt all her defenses collapsing; she was vulnerable and open, but it felt so right.

Then he kissed her, softly at first, but with growing intensity. The world around them instantly disappeared, and Claire lost herself in his kiss.

"Where the hell is she?" Aisha muttered under her breath as she ran around the ballroom, frantically searching for Zoey. After Christopher kissed her, Aisha had immediately scampered off the dance floor, not daring to look in David's direction in case he'd seen her kissing her "cousin." At that point she had planned on dumping Christopher with Claire so that she could go back to David, but she discovered Claire was off in la-la land with Aaron. Now she would need Zoey to take care of him.

"Aha! There you are," Aisha said, grabbing Zoey by the elbow. "I've been looking for you all over the place."

"Why?" Zoey said irritably. "Aren't you busy enough as it is?"

Aisha ignored her friend's tone. "I desperately need your help."

"I told you," Zoey said. "I don't want to be involved in your little game. I have my own problems."

"Why?" Aisha said, momentarily forgetting the urgency of her own situation. "What happened?"

"Yeah, right," Zoey scoffed. "Like you didn't see Lucas make a complete idiot of himself . . . *and* me. It'll probably be on the eleven o'clock news."

"Oh. That."

"And he's been following me around all night," Zoey said tightly. "He just won't leave me alone!"

"Look," Aisha said, trying to sound assertive, "I just need you to distract Christopher for a little while. He's sitting—"

"Let's see—manipulative scheming. Isn't that Claire's job?" Zoey said, cutting her off.

"Well, it turns out Claire's a little busy right now," Aisha muttered, glancing over at the dance floor, where Claire and Aaron were locked in an embrace. "I think she's forgotten about me."

"Sorry, Eesh," Zoey said, shaking her head. "I'm in no mood."

"Zo, Christopher doesn't know anyone," Aisha whined. "You've *got* to talk to him. He's over at that table." Aisha pointed.

"Yeah. Yeah," Zoey said sourly. "I'll go say hi to him because he's my friend. But I am *not* getting involved in any of your craziness. Okay?"

"I'll never forget this, Zo. And whatever you do," Aisha added as she was turning away, "don't let him wander over to the other side of the dance floor."

Aisha ran back to David. So much time had passed since she left him to dance with Christopher that he was definitely going to be pissed. Aisha crossed her fingers and held her breath as she strode up to him. There was a chance that he'd seen her kissing Christopher, too.

"I'm so sorry, David," she said. "That took longer than I thought."

"It's all right," he said, turning to look at her, "but what the hell's going on, Eesh?"

"Nothing," Aisha quickly responded. "It's just that I, ah . . . I mean, my contact lens popped out, and I had to find it, then rush to the bathroom."

"Whatever," he said angrily. "Just don't disappear on me again. Okay?"

"Okay. Sorry." Aisha sat down next to him, relieved that the kiss had escaped his notice.

"So, anyway," David said, his tone changing back to normal, "Dan knows the guy who won the Westinghouse scholarship, Eesh."

Aisha pulled herself together and made a real effort to concentrate on the conversation. "Really?" she said. "How strange."

"It's this guy from Connecticut," Dan said. "He goes to school with a friend of mine."

Aisha kept nodding. Under normal circumstances,

she would have asked a million questions about the guy who beat her out of a college scholarship, but at the moment she had too much else to worry about—like whether Zoey was in any kind of shape to make conversation with Christopher, and how she was going to get away from David again.

"He's really smart, but a real pill, my friend says," Dan went on.

"A pill?" Aisha said disinterestedly.

"Apparently he's unbelievably obnoxious," Dan said. "Nobody likes him."

The band suddenly stopped playing, and the piercing screech of electronic feedback from a microphone stopped all conversation in the ballroom. Aisha covered her ears, shielding them from the painful sound.

Jill Pride, the student body president, walked out onto the center of the dance floor. "May I have your attention, please?" she said into a handheld microphone. Gradually the room fell completely silent, and all eyes were on Jill. "I am very proud to announce this year's prom king and queen."

Twenty

Zoey looked over at Christopher, whose attention was riveted on Jill Pride. *Thank God for prom ceremonies,* she thought. At least now she didn't have the burden of having to make small talk with Christopher, who hadn't done anything to deserve her sourness.

It had been a really long, horrible night for Zoey. She'd actually believed that she could go to the prom and still have fun without Lucas. God knows she'd really tried to have fun, and she'd probably *looked* like she was having fun—but the truth was, she was having a truly lousy time.

Lucas had apologized again and again about invading her privacy, but how could Zoey forgive him? What he'd done was inexcusable and *stupid,* and she wanted to teach him a lesson once and for all.

Jill was thanking everyone who had helped organize the prom, and it seemed as if the list was endless. Finally she got around to the part everyone was waiting for. "We had a very close race this year," she said, "and so many excellent candidates. But unfortunately we can only have one king and one queen." She paused, collecting her thoughts. "We'd like to honor this year's prom king for overcoming difficult odds.

When he first joined our class, many of our classmates shunned him and distrusted him . . ."

Which loser is this? Zoey wondered.

". . . because of a serious mistake he made two years ago. But in spite of all these hardships, he thrived and gradually became one of the best-liked seniors." Jill paused again. "The 1999 king of the senior prom is . . ." The drummer gamely did a drumroll. "Lucas Cabral!"

The audience burst into wild applause, though one or two people booed.

Lucas? Prom king?

"Lucas, please come forward," Jill said, smiling. She waited a few seconds, and Zoey heard a few whispers from the audience. "Lucas?" she said again. "Please come forward, Lucas."

Finally Zoey saw some movement in one corner of the ballroom as Lucas started to move slowly toward the dance floor. He looked shocked and almost scared, and when they turned the spotlight on him, Zoey noted that he was beet red.

He took his place next to Jill, looking totally out of place. Zoey almost felt sorry for him. She knew he hated this sort of thing. But another part of her was actually enjoying his discomfort and humiliation. Trina Parsons, a senior and one of the prom organizers, slipped a beauty-pageant-style sash around him that said Prom King 1999. Lucas turned crimson.

As Zoey was watching all of this, it occurred to her that she might actually be elected queen; they sometimes tried to vote couples as prom king and queen. Suddenly her palms were sweating, and she found herself crossing her fingers and holding her breath.

"And now for Lucas's queen," Jill said. "This year's prom queen is a popular and well-respected member of the student body. She's not only bright and beautiful, but she's also one of the most promising writers in our class. I am very proud to announce that this year's prom queen is . . ." Another drumroll. "Zoey Passmore!"

Zoey let her breath out. She was queen!

The audience applauded enthusiastically, and Christopher squeezed Zoey's shoulder as she got up from her chair. Everyone around her was looking at her and smiling. "Go, Zoey!" someone said as she pushed her way through to the dance floor.

Trina Parsons pinned a sash around her and placed a heavy crown on her head. Suddenly Zoey realized she was beaming as she waved to all her classmates, and the audience was whistling, hooting, and clapping loudly. *This is an honor,* she thought, *and I won't let Lucas spoil it.*

"Congratulations to both of you!" Jill Pride said into the microphone. "And now, everyone, please step back to make way for our king and queen." Zoey looked at Jill, uncertain what to do. "You guys have to dance," Jill whispered to Zoey and Lucas.

Lucas took a hesitant step toward Zoey, and Zoey looked at him warily. She was still pissed off at him, and the last thing she wanted to do was dance with him in front of all these people.

The band started playing, and Zoey immediately recognized the song: Elton John's "Can You Feel the Love Tonight." *It sure isn't love I'm feeling tonight,* Zoey thought as she watched Lucas take another tentative step toward her.

He half opened his arms, waiting for her to give him some sign of encouragement. Zoey sighed resignedly, then forced herself to move forward. Lucas gently took one of her hands in his and placed his other hand on the small of her back. In spite of herself, Zoey began to soften at his touch.

He betrayed your trust, Zoey. Don't give in, she told herself. *Fight back. You've got to show him.*

Lucas tipped his head forward at a slight angle and pressed his cheek against hers.

You're mad at him. He's got no integrity.

He took her hand and rested it on his chest. Zoey could feel his heartbeat. She could smell his familiar scent.

If you give in now, he'll think you've forgiven him.

He was standing so close, Zoey could feel his hips brushing against hers. She resisted the urge to move in tandem with him.

No. Do not melt. Do not pass go. Do not collect two hundred dollars, she told herself.

Suddenly he was kissing her deeply, his lips lush and delicious. And Zoey was kissing him back, all her anger melting away.

Zoey was vaguely aware of the audience hooting and whistling in the background, but the sounds seemed so far away. She closed her eyes and deafened her ears. She didn't want anything to interfere with the incredible sensation of Lucas's mouth on hers. She wanted the kiss to go on forever.

Aisha watched in distress as Zoey and Lucas danced. (Well, it wasn't exactly dancing. It was more like kissing while standing up and swaying from side to side.) Now what? Who was going to distract Christopher? She scanned the ballroom again, praying for a solution. Claire had disappeared from the scene entirely. And now Zoey was in la-la land, too.

Aisha gasped as she noticed Christopher get up and begin circling the room. He seemed to be looking for her. Thinking quickly, she grabbed her purse and stood up, intending to get to him before he got to her.

"David," she said, tapping his shoulder, "I'll be right back. I have to go to the bathroom."

"Again?" David said incredulously. "Either you have a very small bladder or something's wrong." He looked at her closely. "Is everything all right?"

Christopher was coming nearer and nearer, but he didn't seem to have spotted her yet. "Yes, yes," she said to David hurriedly. "But I've got to go."

She stepped backward, but David tugged on her hand. "Wait. I have to go, too."

"But I have to go *now!*" Aisha said, panicking. "Just let me go. Please." Christopher was perilously close to them now. He would see her any second. Aisha snatched her hand away from David, then turned around and headed for the door as fast as she could. *Forget them both,* she said to herself. *It's time to make a French exit.*

"What's the matter with you?" David called after her.

Aisha hesitated for a moment, debating whether or not to turn around. No, she decided. She kept on going, hoping that he wouldn't follow her.

But just as she reached the door David caught up to her. "Aisha, why are you acting like this?" he said, taking her by the shoulders and making her face him. "It's so weird."

Over David's shoulder, Aisha made eye contact with Christopher. He was smiling and waving to her from about six feet away. Aisha opened her mouth to speak, but no words came out.

"Hey! Where've you been?" Christopher said as he approached. "I've been looking everywhere for you."

"Uh, hi," Aisha squeaked. "I've been looking for you, too."

David glanced over his shoulder. "Oh, hi," he said to Christopher. "You must be Aisha's cousin."

Christopher gave him a befuddled look. "Cousin?"

"Um, David," Aisha said before David could say anything. "This is Christopher."

"Nice to meet you," David said, offering his hand.

"Nice to meet you, too." Christopher shook his hand, then looked at him closely. "Wait a minute," he said as though he was trying to remember something. "Haven't I met you before?"

David shook his head. "No, I don't think so."

"Wait a minute," Christopher said again, pointing his finger at David.

Aisha stepped back, cringing.

"I know you." Christopher's voice was hard, and he was scowling. "You're that skeezer who was kissing Aisha in front of her house!"

David looked at Aisha. "Who *is* this guy?"

Aisha covered her face with her hands and shook her head from side to side. She felt her world caving in around her. She had never imagined that Christopher would recognize David from that night.

"I'm her boyfriend," Christopher said, advancing toward David aggressively. "Who are you?"

"So this is Christopher," David said softly.

Aisha looked at David mournfully. She didn't know what to say. "I'm so sorry," she said, choking up. "I'm so sorry."

"Eesh, how could you?" David's mouth was trembling.

Aisha shook her head mutely. She didn't have any answers.

"Well, I'm sorry, too," David said, his voice full of emotion. "I guess it's finished." He pushed open the door to leave, and Aisha didn't stop him. What could she say to him to make it all right?

Christopher was staring at her intently. "You told me

you weren't seeing him anymore," he said harshly. "You told me it was over! You lied to me, Eesh. How could you lie to me?"

Aisha looked down at her feet. "I *did* stop seeing him," she whispered. "But I had already promised to go to the prom with him, and I just couldn't let him down."

"What?" Christopher said angrily. "What the hell does that mean?"

"He asked me to the prom before you came to town."

"And *you* asked *me* to the prom, if you recall," he said sarcastically. "What were you thinking?"

Aisha struggled to find an explanation, but she was too confused and upset to think.

"Aisha, I think I deserve an explanation." He put his hand under her chin and lifted her face up to him. "Look at me."

Tears were streaming down Aisha's cheeks. "I don't have any explanations," she said hoarsely. "I'm sorry."

Christopher shook his head regretfully. "I don't think I can ever trust you again, Eesh. And without trust, our relationship is worthless."

"Please, Christopher," Aisha said. "I know what I did was wrong—and I'm sorry. But give me another chance."

Christopher shut his eyes as though he was in pain. "I'm sorry, Eesh," he said. "But I just can't."

"Please, Christopher," she begged. "All I want is to be with you. I love you." Aisha reached out to touch his cheek. Her own face was wet with tears.

Christopher turned his head away. "Don't," he said coldly. "I can't bear to have you touch me."

Twenty-one

Nina hopped onto one of the bar-style stools at Niko's, an outdoor food stand two blocks away from the inn where she'd been staying since Wednesday night. Behind the counter, a middle-aged man in a food-stained apron was frying some onions and sausages, squinting to protect his eyes from the smoke.

"Hi, Niko," Nina shouted over the roar of the exhaust fan.

Niko looked up. "Nina!" he said with a cigarette hanging from the corner of his mouth. "I'll be with you in a sec." He stabbed one of the sausages with a large cooking fork and placed it in a bun, then piled a lot of onions on top of it. He wrapped some waxed paper around the bottom of the bun and gave the sandwich to a man sitting two stools away from Nina.

"It's your third night in a row here," he said, smiling at Nina and wiping his hands with a towel. "I'm flattered."

"You've got the best gyros in town," Nina said. "But then again, I've never tried any other gyros." Nina had become a regular at Niko's, partly because it was so near the inn and partly because she enjoyed talking to Niko.

"But you're late tonight," Niko observed.

"Yeah," Nina said. "I fell asleep and woke up starving. Thank God you're open till ten. Nothing else is."

Niko nodded in agreement. "This neighborhood is pretty dead after nine. In fact," he said, glancing down at his watch, "you should watch yourself going home. The streets are pretty empty."

"Don't worry about me," Nina said. "With this hairdo"—she pointed to her dyed red hair, which was sticking up in all directions—"even the toughest criminals wouldn't dare come near me."

Niko laughed. "Okay. Just be careful." He pointed to a blackboard behind him. "So what will it be tonight? The usual?"

Nina nodded. "That would make me very happy."

"You got it," Niko said, turning back to his work station.

Nina watched as he expertly made her gyro, her hunger growing more and more acute. She'd spent the day walking all over the old seaport neighborhood, Strawbery Banke, looking at some of the restored eighteenth-century architecture. She hadn't bothered to stop and eat.

Almost as soon as he put the gyro in front of her, she polished it off. "That was the best one yet," she said to Niko as she left three dollars and hopped off the stool. "Thanks a lot."

"You're welcome," he said. "See you tomorrow?"

"Absolutely," Nina said, waving.

"Bye—and be careful!"

Nina walked quickly down the street toward the inn, digging into her pockets for her usual after-dinner cigarette. "Damn," she said, realizing that she'd left her Lucky Strikes on a park bench earlier in the day. She looked up and down the street for some kind of newsstand or convenience store, but there was nothing.

Then she remembered having seen a 7-Eleven a few blocks away, toward the center of town. She stopped to orient herself for a moment, then decided to turn right at the next corner.

A block and a half later, Nina saw the familiar red, white, and green sign all lit up. She smiled. Her sense of direction had improved dramatically since she'd left Chatham Island. It was all just a matter of exercising that part of her brain, which had probably atrophied from living in a small town all her life.

She pushed open the glass door, noticing a group of men half hidden in the shadows edging the small parking area. *What a bunch of losers,* Nina thought. *Don't they have anything better to do than hang out in a parking lot on a Saturday night?* But she had to admit that they sounded like they were having a good time, laughing and shouting raucously. *But then I'm not one to talk. At least they're having fun.*

Nina grabbed a small bag of Doritos from one of the aisles, then went up to the cashier. "A pack of Lucky Strikes, please," she said, slipping a hand into her back pocket for some cash.

The cashier threw a red-and-white pack on the counter. "Anything else?"

"Hey, Lucky Strikes," a man said, setting down a six-pack of beer on the counter. "You're my kind of woman."

Nina looked at him. He was wearing a black motorcycle jacket with silver zippers, torn blue jeans, and heavy black boots. He had too little hair on his head and too much on the rest of his body, judging from the density of hair on the backs of his hands. Probably in his late twenties, she guessed, noticing wiry black chest hair sticking out from under his flannel shirt. "Your brand, too?" she said.

"Yup." He looked her up and down, making Nina

suddenly feel small and self-conscious. Her hair looked as though it hadn't been washed in days, and she had gyro sauce all over her army-surplus pants. "Wait a minute," he said, as if there was something wrong with the picture. "How old are you?"

Nina bristled at his patronizing tone. "Sixteen," she said belligerently.

"Well, little lady, you shouldn't be smoking," he said, smirking. "It'll stunt your growth."

"Thanks for your heartfelt concern," Nina answered sarcastically. "But I don't see how it's any of your business."

"Three sixty-five," the cashier said to Nina.

Nina handed her a five-dollar bill, consciously avoiding the man's eyes.

"Well, *sorry,* little lady," the man said condescendingly. "I just thought you might want to get to be over five feet some day."

Nina bit her tongue. This guy was a jerk. She should just take her change and leave. She took the change from the cashier, said thank you, then headed for the door, all the while keeping her comments to herself. But just as she got to the exit something inside her snapped, and she slowly turned around and looked him straight in the eye. "I might not be tall," she said, "but at least I don't look like I just fell into a vat of pubic hair."

The man's face contorted into an angry scowl. "You little bitch!" she heard him call as she stepped out into the parking lot.

Nina broke into a run. Insulting the stranger had been a stupid thing to do even though he deserved it, she realized.

Suddenly someone grabbed her from behind. "Where do you think you're going?" a man said, pinning her arms to her sides.

"Let me go!" Nina screamed. She tried to move her arms and kick, but the man overpowered her. "Let me go!"

Claire floated all the way up Lighthouse Road toward home. "I've totally flipped," she said aloud. "I'm so in love with him, I'm talking to myself." She laughed softly to herself. Never in her life had she felt so giddy, so absolutely elated—not even the first time she fell for him.

After that first, intense kiss on the dance floor, she and Aaron had held each other for a long, long time, both of them oblivious to what was going on around them. They had clung to each other almost desperately, until finally someone had asked them to clear the floor for the prom king and queen awards. From there they had found the hotel spa, where they spent the rest of the evening making up for lost time.

Right there on the spa carpet, among all the gym equipment, they had kissed and held each other until two in the morning.

Now it was nearly three-thirty, but Claire didn't feel the least bit tired. Her skin was still tingling from his touch, and her lips still tasted sweet from his kisses. It had been so difficult to part ways at the dock, where the water taxi had dropped them off. But they still had till six the next day to be together. Then, sadly, he would have to go back to school.

Claire noticed that the light was on in her father's study. She opened the front door as quietly as she could, praying that he wasn't waiting up for her. She had promised to be home by two.

"Claire?" she heard as she stepped in. Her heart sank. Her father was up.

"Hi, it's me," she said, cautiously poking her head into the study.

"I'm glad you're home, honey," he said. He looked older, almost withered.

"I'm sorry I'm late," she said.

"Oh, it's all right," he said gently. "I'm just glad you're safe."

Claire wondered why her father had let her off so easily. He was usually pretty strict with her and Nina about curfews. "Is everything all right?" Claire asked, going over to his side. "You don't look well."

"Claire," her father said raggedly, "Sarah left me today."

The statement, so simple and to the point, sliced right through Claire's heart. Two seconds earlier she had been on top of the world, but now she felt herself plummeting. She hurt on behalf of her father, but mostly she felt the pain of knowing that *she* was responsible for his misery. She felt tears come to her eyes. "I'm so sorry, Dad." *More sorry than you could possibly know.*

"But please don't worry," he told her. "It'll work out."

Claire took his hand, struggling to find the words to comfort him. It amazed her that she had never even stopped to consider the emotional repercussions when she had devised her evil plan. So urgent had been her need to banish Aaron from her life that she had barely even thought of what it would do to her father. Now, face-to-face with her father's grief, she wished that she had never gone through with it. And she wished more than anything that she could bring Sarah back. For his sake.

"It *will* work out," she said, promising herself that she would find a way to undo the damage she had done. "I promise you. It will."

Making Out:
Zoey speaks out

Book 18 in the explosive series about broken hearts, secrets, friendship, and of course, love.

Jake will never forgive **Kate** for standing him up, although it was **Lara's** fault. **Lara** is desperate to keep **Jake** for herself, and unless **Lucas** tells **Zoey** what really happened, **Kate** and **Jake** will stay apart. It's a brave decision when ...

Zoey
speaks
out

A fantasy, a love story, a summer of change...

The China Garden

By LIZ BERRY

AVON
tempest

"Like a jewel box with hidden drawers and
compartments, this finely crafted, multilayered
novel holds many secrets...richly laden with
mystery and suspense, in which the ordinary
often masks unexpected interconnections
and the extraordinary is natural to the story's
wildly imagined terrain."
—PUBLISHERS WEEKLY ☆

CHN 0599

READ ONE...READ THEM ALL—
The Hot New Series about Falling in Love

MAKING OUT
by KATHERINE APPLEGATE

(#1) **Zoey fools around**	80211-2 /$3.99 US/$5.50 Can
(#2) **Jake finds out**	80212-0/$3.99 US/$4.99 Can
(#3) **Nina won't tell**	80213-9/$3.99 US/$4.99 Can
(#4) **Ben's in love**	80214-7/$3.99 US/$4.99 Can
(#5) **Claire gets caught**	80215-5/$3.99 US/$5.50 Can
(#6) **What Zoey saw**	80216-3/$3.99 US/$4.99 Can
(#7) **Lucas gets hurt**	80217-1 /$3.99 US/$4.99 Can
(#8) **Aisha goes wild**	80219-8/$3.99 US/$4.99 Can
(#9) **Zoey plays games**	80742-4/$3.99 US/$4.99 Can
(#10) **Nina shapes up**	80743-2/$3.99 US/$5.50 Can
(#11) **Ben takes a chance**	80867-6/$3.99 US/$5.50 Can
(#12) **Claire can't lose**	80868-4/$3.99 US/$5.50 Can
(#13) **Don't tell Zoey**	80869-2/$3.99 US/$5.50 Can
(#14) **Aaron lets go**	80870-6/$3.99 US/$5.50 Can
(#15) **Who loves Kate?**	80871-4/$3.99 US/$5.50 Can
(#16) **Lara gets even**	80872-2/$3.99 US/$5.50 Can

Love stories just a little more perfect than real life...

Don't miss any in the

enchanted ♥ HEARTS

series:

♥ 1 The Haunted Heart   by Cherie Bennett

♥ 2 Eternally Yours   by Jennifer Baker

♥ 3 Lost and Found   by Cameron Dokey

♥ 4 Love Potion   by Janet Quin-Harkin

♥ 5 Spellbound   by Phyllis Karas

♥ 6 Love Him Forever   by Cherie Bennett

ehs 0499